Aristotle's Wolves

ATLANTIS
BOOK TWO

COURTNEY DAVIS

5 PRINCE PUBLISHING

Published by 5 PRINCE PUBLISHING & BOOKS, LLC

PO Box 865, Arvada, CO 80001

www.5PrinceBooks.com

ISBN digital: 978-1-63112-348-1

ISBN print: 978-1-63112-349-8

Cover Credit: Marianne Nowicki

F10242023

To my loving husband.
I will never underestimate the value of your
support in this adventure.
You make my writing dream possible.

Acknowledgments

Thank you to the team at 5 Prince Publishing for their continued belief in my writing and for Cate Byers, you are amazing. I am a better writer after every interaction with you.

Other Titles by

COURTNEY DAVIS

The Atlantis Series

The Vampires of Atlantis

Aristotle's Wolves

Descendants of Atlantis

The Serpent and the Firefly

A Spider in the Garden

Princess of Prias

Aristotle's Wolves

One

LILLY PACED in the small cage; her mind splintered. She never allowed herself to remember her other form; she couldn't, it was far too painful. This was all she was now; all she would ever be. It was easier to accept it, to just not think at all. She paced, she slept, and sometimes she ate.

If she forgot to keep it from her mind, she would remember that she wanted to run, to hunt and shift. She had no idea how long it had been since she was out on a hunt of any kind.

How long since she'd last breathed fresh air?

How long since she'd seen another of her own kind?

She wondered if the vampires were gone, was she a useless tool now? A dusty weapon set aside?

Most days she paced in the small space until her legs were ready to give out and this kept her mind from remembering. She paced until the sweet release of darkness swam over her eyes. Was it hunger, or was it exhaustion? She didn't know, but she welcomed it because for a time, she could just dream and in her dreams she was free.

When her eyes opened again, the smell of her own waste mixed with dampness and mildew hit her. She remembered where she was, and she wished desperately to go back to sleep where she could join her pack on a hunt under the full moon, or walk on two legs along a street packed with people. Anything but this. She fought to keep the panic down and pushed her mind to suppress reality. But so often she couldn't completely forget, couldn't force her mind into that place where it just existed without recognition, without past or future.

What kind of future could she possibly hope for at this point? She wished for death some days. But she couldn't die of old age or slow starvation, not even silver poisoning apparently. Her body was too strong, it fought too hard to stay alive and she resented it more often than not.

She was in a cage; she would likely never leave it. The only measure of time passing was the once a week when the water pipes set around the room turned on for thirty minutes and flushed the floor clean. She would stand as the water swirled around her ankles, pushing her waste to the drain outside of the cage and into the sewer. She would close her eyes and breathe in the smell of cool water, remembering days spent jumping into rivers, catching fish in her jaws. It was impossible to keep the memories away on those days, impossible not to mourn all that she'd lost.

Even when he came down and tossed her some kind of scrap, she was often able to stay disassociated, to experience it as if it were someone else. This wasn't her life, it couldn't be.

Today was not a water day and so far it didn't seem like it was going to be a food day either. She'd paced as long as she could before she circled twice, then laid down with her black tail over her snout. The smell of her own fur was comforting.

Lilly's mind wandered as she waited for sleep. All the way back to when she'd been young and hopeful. Running through fields alongside her father. He was the biggest werewolf she'd ever seen. Deep red fur with a streak of white along his back and bright blue eyes. He was much faster than her of course, he would circle her as she ran laughing and pointing out the rabbits they were scaring up.

He would chase them down and lope back to her with the fresh kill in his big jaws.

She put them in her sack to carry home and they would continue on. This was her favorite way to gather dinner and for a girl of ten, it felt like the most normal thing in the world.

Which is why when she'd turned eighteen, she had decided that she must become one too. That there was no life she wanted to live more than the one her father and his pack led. No matter the risk.

"I'm the daughter of a strong alpha," she stated proudly. "I have your blood running through my veins and I will survive the change."

Her father had said no every time she'd asked for an entire year. But on her nineteenth birthday he could no longer deny her request, especially after she threatened to go to another pack and have another alpha change her.

"My sweet, Lilly Flower, I can't lose you," he begged. "When your mother didn't make it through, you're the only thing that kept me sane."

"I'm stronger than she ever was, you know I am. She didn't have alpha blood in her veins, that has to make a difference."

She was stubborn and he could see it in her eyes.

And so, against his better judgment, he agreed.

He sent the pack away, didn't want anyone else around when she changed, or to stop him if she died and he decided to follow her into the afterlife.

She'd taken on this life hoping to rule beside her father and take over the pack when he was gone. She'd wanted to run free with the pack and experience life in a way others could only dream of. Any fear of not making it through the change was far outweighed by the benefits she saw in living life as a werewolf.

She was now a wolf in form, but she wasn't living a werewolf life, hadn't breathed air outside of this basement in so long, she wasn't sure she remembered what it smelled like. Struggled to recall grass under her paws or the rip of flesh and bone in her jaws. Running, jumping, playing, fucking... they were all things she hadn't experienced in so long that a part of her had decided they weren't real. All that was real was this barred cell, those awful men, the shit, and the chains.

Sometimes there was meat.

She popped her head up, all thoughts of sleep suddenly gone as she heard the unmistakable sound of five bolts and locks being undone. The door opened at the top of the stairs. He was coming and that meant it was a day she would eat. Her nose told her it was the one in charge this time, Brandon. Brandon smelled like sweat and fear. Glen, the other one, was too stupid to smell like fear. He smelled like sweat and grease. They both trickled an odor that stung her nose, something toxic and she wondered if they were intentionally poisoning themselves with the substance. She wondered if eventually they would just not come.

How long after they both died would she remain in this cage before someone discovered her? And if some random human did discover her, would they kill her thinking they were doing her a favor, putting the poor beast out of its misery. She probably looked diseased and half dead.

They would probably be right. Death would be a sweet release from her current situation.

Brandon reached the bottom of the staircase and today she had the presence of mind to react. She let out a low vicious growl.

"Shut up, bitch!" Brandon snapped and waved a gun in her direction. "You're finally going to live up to your purpose."

She bared her teeth at him, but she stopped growling, daring to hope that she was going to get out, that she was about to be slipped from the silver chains holding her back. They had been on so long the fur was rubbed completely off in places and her skin left raw underneath. She'd been vain in her youth, so proud to be a wolf of pure black, not a speck of other color on her so she could blend seamlessly with the night. She'd been perfectly muscled and able to run for hours without being winded.

She hated to think what she looked like now, luckily there was no one to impress.

When she'd first turned, she had of course drawn the notice of every male in the pack just for being a female werewolf.

They had thought she was a female that they didn't have to hold back with, a female that could give and take with a male werewolf with equal ferocity. They thought she was someone perhaps who could carry a child for them and birth something greater than any of them.

Not for her lack of trying, and others', she was never able to carry a child. The forced change of the full moon was too violent, too complete. No fetus could survive that. She was thankful now, after everything she'd been through. She couldn't imagine what her life would have been like if she'd had children either before or during her captivity.

Brandon walked over to a freezer and pulled out a frozen steak. "You want this? I'll give you one now and one tonight after you take down a bloodsucker. Think about it all day and remember what your big ass teeth are supposed to do," he sneered and shoved the steak through the bars.

She didn't move to eat it, just stared at him. He huffed and turned, walking back up the stairs. She heard the door shut and all five locks click back into place. Only then did she walk over to the freezer-burned meat and eat it in two bites. It wasn't good, but she knew she needed the strength, especially if what he said was true.

Would she really get a chance to leave this cage tonight? Could she get away from him if she did? Could she signal for help? Would there be anyone to signal? The possibilities dared her to hope for things she thought she'd given up on a long time ago.

Lilly was on edge all day, ears perked and body tense. Every noise upstairs had her jumping to attention and listening. Was he coming? Was it now? Would the sun set and her dreams of fresh air be quashed?

What if he wasn't lying, what if he did let her out and they came across a vampire? Did she have the strength to do what she needed to do? Did she remember how to take one down, would her instincts kick in?

Two

HER MIND DRIFTED BACK in time. Back before the railroads reached across the United States. She'd been raised on the east coast. Her father had been bitten by his uncle, Titus, as a young man, never aging beyond what looked like his mid-twenties. Titus had no male children of his own and so had taken her father on as his heir. He had changed him and taught him how to run the pack, how to be a fair and fierce alpha. Titus had been a very respected man in the werewolf community and so her father, Roald, had been as well. Wealthy, powerful, and smart, both of them. When Titus died there was no question about who would take over, no challenge made against Roald. He was alpha and he was good at it.

Her mother, Cindy, had been a human of course. She had fallen in love with the man that Roald presented himself to be without knowing what secrets he kept hidden. At that point, Roald had been a werewolf for nearly thirty years and alpha for ten. He wanted a family and saw Cindy as a perfect candidate because she was a woman on her own, no family in the area to ask questions about a husband who didn't age. He'd wooed her and proposed to her before revealing what he truly was. He wasn't a monster, he didn't marry her first, just made sure she was well and truly in love before revealing his other side. Roald told Lilly that her mother had been shocked initially, but more intrigued than scared and she had quickly agreed to a life lived with a werewolf husband.

After Cindy gave birth to Lilly, she decided she didn't want more children, didn't want to age beyond what her husband looked like. She wanted to risk the change sooner rather than later. She refused to have more children, said that if Roald wouldn't change her, she would leave him and take Lilly with her to live a normal life. She couldn't stand by aging while her husband stayed frozen in time.

It was something even Roald couldn't ask her to do, so he agreed.

The change was difficult, painful, and violent. Cindy hadn't survived and at four, Lilly had been left alone with her father and his pack. It could have been a rough situation, but the pack loved her like their own daughters. She'd felt loved and cherished as she'd grown up with what felt like a dozen uncles and aunts. She didn't think she'd missed out on anything not having her mother around, but maybe she had.

Roald's love for Cindy kept him from marrying again, never engendering another child, but Lilly had other kids of the pack to play with, so she didn't mind being an only child. On full moon nights she was locked safely in the basement along with any other wives or children of the pack that were at the packhouse. They had to be kept where no werewolf could harm them during that change because it was so complete, werewolves often found it difficult to control urges and could so easily harm the ones they loved.

It hadn't taken her long to figure out she didn't want to spend the rest of her life locked away once a month as the wife of a werewolf and she didn't want to marry and have kids with some human who would never know the truth about her father and his pack. So she had made what to her was an obvious decision. She would be changed.

The change was an unforgettable experience. It had been excruciating of course. She'd expected the pain although she hadn't ever witnessed a change. She'd heard the stories plenty of times and her father had used it to try and dissuade her. The bites were bad. Three deep chomps had to be given to ensure enough venom passed into her bloodstream. It raced through her system like fire and her body broke into a million pieces before pulling itself back together. Her bones reformed, her muscles stretched and expanded. Her nerves grew and sensitized.

The change rippled over her body, and she screamed; she wanted to die in those moments, wanted to change her mind. She would marry a nice human boy, she would have his children, and she would never talk about her childhood with a pack of were-wolves. If only the pain would stop.

Just as she was about to give up, to go to the black emptiness hidden in the pain, her eyes focused on her father. He was standing over her and behind his fear for her, she saw a pride that filled her with determination to survive.

She wanted to live for him, wanted him to be proud of how strong she was.

That's when she heard it, the call of death. She saw the cloaked woman stand before her and offer relief at a single touch.

"I heard your call, and I can stop it all, forever," Death beckoned.

"No," Lilly whispered as another round of pain swept her into a frenzy of violent shudders. She clamped her eyes shut, losing sight of her father but not the strength his presence was giving her. "No, I will survive this, and I will become a wolf to make my father proud." Lilly opened her eyes and stared Death in the face.

Death shed her cloak and stood before Lilly. Not a skeleton, not a human. She had the upper body and head of a wolf, with fur that seamlessly flowed into the fabric of a dress covering her to her feet. Her bare human feet. She had arms covered in fur, and delicate human hands. Her eyes were a bright glowing red and she walked over to Lilly gracefully.

She whispered in Lilly's ear. "You have my blessing to cheat death, you are strong, use it well. You'll need it for yourself and for him. Survive."

Death disappeared as Lilly's face broke, she couldn't breathe momentarily while her mouth and nose reformed into a snout. She was blinded as her eyes grew and changed.

And then it was done.

She panted and the scents that came to her were sharp and filled her brain with the knowledge of everything surrounding her. Her eyes opened and she saw, clear as if it were day, her father there, watching with careful concern.

I will be strong for you, she promised silently.

When she got up, wobbly at first on her four legs, it was as if the forest stood silent. Watching, waiting.

Then she howled, her father howled, and off in the distance the pack answered with howls of their own, it was music to her ears. They came running on silent paws, she could feel the connection, knew that this was her family.

As they each stepped through into the clearing, they first darted their eyes cautiously to her father, silently asking permission to be there. Roald stood stoic, he didn't acknowledge them, but he allowed them to stay, to be there and witness her. Each one then eyed her with a glint that made her cautious, she had known that she would have to prove herself against them, knew she'd have to make them see that she was just as strong, just as fast as any male.

Now she understood that she would need that proof of strength to keep herself safe from them. As more and more wolves entered the clearing, she understood what her father had been too afraid to tell her.

They would all want her, and if anyone challenged her father and won, she could end up taken, or given, by any alpha who took over the pack. But as long as her father was in charge, they would all treat her with respect, or suffer his wrath. She would have to be strong for both of them.

She held her head high as they gathered around and reminded herself that she was one of them, blessed by the great spirit of death to walk the earth as a wolf and human, protecting it from those monsters who would dare to harm its most precious children. If they didn't respect her because she had a goddamn vagina, then she was prepared to rip out a few throats to prove herself.

She bared her teeth at them and waited for a challenge, to her or her father. No one stepped forward and as the last of the pack entered the clearing, her father shifted to human and stood proudly beside her.

"My pack, welcome our newest member," he shouted, motioning to her. "She is to be treasured and protected. She is special," he said, looking at her with a soft smile. When he turned to look each wolf in the eye, he wore an expression of stern commandment. The message was clear, they were to stay away.

They did for the most part. Some tried to woo her, some sniffed around, obviously interested and waiting for her to show interest back. None pressed the issue, and none challenged her father. She was no longer accepted by the wives and daughters, that was the hardest part of her new position in the pack. She was no longer one of their group, she was seen as a threat to their marriages, their happy homes. She was also proof that the change was possible for daughters and wives, not just sons.

Eventually she picked a wolf as a mate. A fair furred young man who'd turned just a few years prior to herself and had broad shoulders and an easy smile, Edward.

Her father had been ecstatic and encouraged the courting. She knew he was mostly excited for her to not be single and would have been equally happy about any werewolf. But she liked Edward and she tried to make it work, she even agreed to try and have a baby with him. There was no way of knowing what the baby would be like, but they were willing to try, willing to birth a child that might come with shifting abilities out of the womb. There were no stories about it happening, no lingering mythology to tell them what to expect. The rumors of past females had barely been believed before she'd succeeded and even those stories never went beyond the female making it through the change.

She vividly remembered that month when her period didn't come, and she ran to her father with glee. She was going to bring something into the world that would no doubt be amazing.

Then the full moon came. She bled through it and when she was once again in her human form she knew. The baby was gone, her hope of ever having a child was gone and the wives looked at her with pity and a bit of malice; they had something she didn't. To them, this meant that Lilly would no longer be prized above a human wife that could bear male children who might one day become a werewolf. She felt like she was less than a male werewolf because she couldn't even impregnate a female human. She would never expand the pack, one of their most pressing instincts.

Not that her father felt that way about her. He didn't allow any others to speak such things, but she saw it there, in their eyes and glances. It was in everything they didn't say to her, and she wondered for the first time if she'd made a mistake becoming this. One thing she had never expected to give up for this life had been ripped away.

While she mourned the loss of the child and the idea of children in the future, Edward left her, left the whole pack. No one else in her father's pack had tried to mate her after that.

But, Lilly supposed, if you could never be a mother, you could never be a bad mother. You could never choose to risk death when your child was so young and leave her before she was ready to be without you. Lilly would never disappoint a child who needed her, because she would never have a child.

Lilly threw herself into the life of a werewolf because what other choice was there? She hunted, fought, and killed a few vampires with her pack. She wanted to protect innocent humans, it was the calling of a werewolf. The reason they existed, and they were good at it. Werewolves may hide in shadows, afraid of being called monsters themselves, but it was worth the trade because they were doing good.

Purpose in life was important. Some found that purpose in building a family, others with art or craft. For her, she was a protector of innocents, destroyer of vampires, and she was good at it.

When she was captured, it wasn't because she'd been stupid, or weak. It was because she'd been tricked. The scent of vampire had drawn her into a trap set by the Aristotle Society. Then she was theirs, broken from her pack. She knew—as soon as the silver pricked into her—what was happening. She'd heard stories, had smelled the captured wolves, and avoided them for fear of becoming one.

Was it youthful stupidity, or maybe overconfidence, that had driven her to chase alone that night? She wasn't sure. Either way, it was a mistake she had paid for, for too many years to count.

"Dear lord, it's a female," one of the captors said as they had slipped a collar around her neck and she felt the cord between herself and her pack cut cleanly off.

A vicious-looking man stepped forward and slipped the matching ring around his own finger, assuring that she was locked to his demands and bound to his life. He had several other rings on his hands as well. He was the leader, and she wasn't his first capture.

"Well, well, well, looks like the boys at home will be having fun tonight. I expect we'll see pups soon," he said darkly.

"Is that how it works?" one of the others asked dumbly.

"Of course it is, you idiot. Don't you know how babies are made?" another answered with a sneer and a laugh.

The leader crouched down and looked into her eyes. She couldn't move, the bullets had sapped her strength so fast. She could feel every part of her body working to push them out so she would survive this, but it left nothing for her to resist with. Not that she could now. The collar made certain of that.

"You unlucky bitch," he said and flicked her nose.

She couldn't help the whine that escaped her, and she hated herself for it. The men had laughed.

Lilly stopped pacing the cage and stared up at the stairwell. She'd hunted with those men and their descendants for years. Watching their numbers dwindle in both men and wolves. Despite the fact that she wasn't shifting from human to wolf anymore, she still wasn't able to keep a pregnancy past the full moon. Which really pissed off the men when they realized it wasn't going to happen. Perhaps the body of a killing machine wasn't able to hold the most precious thing on earth.

It was a blessing then.

Being captive made her question every decision she'd ever made. Wouldn't a short human life have been better than this endless torture and captivity?

Eventually the numbers in the Aristotle Society went to nearly nothing. Now it was just the two idiots upstairs, and her. Those two had never taken her hunting, Brandon's father barely had. She'd already been in this cage for quite a while when Brandon's father had died, still fairly young. Brandon had come down with a smile that day and with the ring on his finger to tell her she was his now, looking no more than eighteen at the time, she'd hoped he would be stupid enough to make a mistake.

Apparently, he was more afraid than stupid because he'd never opened the cage door.

The hope of escape was the only thing that kept her from going completely insane. Though there were times when she may have slipped into insanity, she'd managed to pull herself back out after the loss of unknown amounts of time. Hope was a double-edged sword when you were better off just rolling over and dying.

Living this life was painful, but she just couldn't give up, couldn't let them win. And what if her father was out there, what if he eventually came for her? If he found her dead, it would kill him.

So she continued to be strong and survive for him.

Three

LILLY COULD SENSE the sun setting and she waited anxiously for Brandon to come back down. When he did, she was eager in her mind, but she didn't let her body show anything. She wouldn't let him know how much she was looking forward to getting out of this cage.

Brandon unlocked the door and she felt a thrill run through her. She wanted to destroy this man, but for now she'd settle for fresh air, room to run, and maybe a fresh meal. After all, she wouldn't get a chance to kill him, not with the collar on her and that ring on him.

The collar was more than just a silver-lined thing keeping her from shifting back to human. It was spelled by a witch, binding her to the one who wears the ring. If he died, so would she.

Brandon's great-grandfather wore the ring, then his grandfather, his father for a short time and now him. Her life had been handed down like an inheritance.

She saw fear behind Brandon's eyes as he approached her, but he covered it with false bravado and a grin. He couldn't cover the scent of it though, fear stank like sour milk, and he reeked of it. How was she a possession of such a worthless coward?

"Sit, bitch," he demanded, and she just looked at him.

He pointed the gun at her, and she sat, she didn't trust that he wouldn't actually shoot her. He probably wouldn't kill her, but a bullet would hurt all the same, especially in her weakened condition.

"That's a good girl," he whispered and stepped closer, lowering the weapon and holding up a leash. "We are going hunting, there's a vampire in Miami and we're going to catch it."

There was an eagerness in his voice that she could relate to. He latched the leash to her collar then cautiously unwound the chains from her body.

She winced internally, the sting as the silver pulled from her skin was terrible, but she wouldn't show reaction, wouldn't give him even a hint of weakness.

"You're one tough bitch, I'll give you that," Brandon said when he dropped the last of the chain on the floor.

She looked down at the offending chain. Flesh and hair was embedded in it, melded with the silver after so much time. She compartmentalized the sight into a place she hoped to never look at again.

She lifted her lips in a silent snarl at Brandon, but he wasn't paying attention to her, he was fumbling with his belt. It would be so easy to kill him, he'd deserve it.

He was dressed in jeans and a black shirt, at least he was trying to blend with the night, she supposed. But he had on a ridiculous belt that hung from his slim waist and he kept tugging on it. She wasn't sure what all the things he had there were, but they must be heavy because he kept adjusting and yanking on it. She nearly rolled her eyes as he fidgeted.

A child playing dress-up in his father's clothes, that's what he reminded her of. He'd never survive against a vampire without her.

"Ready to roll, bitch," he said and yanked her leash.

She'd never wanted to bite him more.

As she stepped through the cell doorway she was filled with a sense of urgency. Freedom, fresh air, the chance to scent another werewolf. The urge to bolt was strong, her muscles were tense, and she felt her fur ripple. She had to hold herself steady, had to be smart. If there was a chance for escape she'd take it, but she couldn't risk him putting her back in the cage and not letting her back out because she'd been too eager. She was smart, she could bide her time.

"Up the stairs," he directed as if she didn't understand the goal. She may have been in that cage for years, but she did know how to get out of a damn room.

She hurried up the stairs, feeling the leash hold her back, and into the dust covered store. It was empty of people but stuffed full of various items, some of which she was sure she'd never seen before in her life. It was jarring, to see items that looked old and used but more modern than anything she'd ever encountered. What had changed in the world since the last time she'd been on two feet?

Brandon halted her at the door that led out to the street. She looked up at him expectantly. She was ready, she could already smell the fresh air pushing through the gaps in the door. She wanted out but was afraid to pull too aggressively on the leash, afraid he'd reconsider, and she'd find herself back in that cell without even getting any farther than this.

She thought she might turn and rip out his throat if he tried that, end this suffering for both of them.

"We need to be careful," he murmured and once again fiddled with the items around his belt. "We can't be seen by anyone. Animal control will be up my ass if they find out I've got a wolf in the city. Luckily, you're small enough to be a large dog and you look like shit, honestly. You're an ugly thing."

She let out a small growl. It was his fault she looked like this, malnourished as she was and because of those damn chains. She could already feel her body straining to heal the wounds now that most of the silver had been removed.

"Stay hidden so I don't have to put you down." He spun the ring on his finger, and she shivered. The ring assured that she would try to protect him with her life because he was the weakest thing about her. He could also draw from her magic to heal his own wounds as long as he wore it. She wondered if that was another reason she felt so weak. Was her healing magic being constantly pulled to him, an obviously unhealthy human?

He reached around her and pulled the door open. She drew in great gulps of fresh air and nearly choked on the myriad smells. The city scent was unfamiliar after so long and she sneezed as her sensitive nose was overwhelmed.

They stepped out onto the darkened street. Streetlights lit up the scene that was both familiar and not. There were people all around, walking up and down everywhere. Brandon had wanted her to stay hidden, but he hadn't waited long enough after sunset to take her out apparently. Some of the people they passed commented on what an ugly dog she was. She had to admit, it hurt, she'd always been so proud of her beautiful fur. But Brandon was probably right, it helped to distract from what she really was. No one looked too closely at a sickly dog on a leash, but that might not hold true for long. Knowing that she had to be the smart one, she led him to the dark safety of an alleyway to cloak them.

"Good girl," Brandon said with a slight shake to his voice.

His adrenaline was no doubt high, he was probably riding it, feeling powerful. She wished she could tell him what she saw in him. A scared and stupid, weak human, who didn't deserve the honor of a werewolf at his side.

Not all of the wolves belonging to the Aristotle Society had traditionally been imprisoned like her. Some had gone willingly into a symbiotic relationship with The Society at first. They had worked together and driven vampires to the shadows, or so the legend said.

Long after the city sank and the vampires took the beasts below the waterline, the werewolves had ruled on land. Then some bloodsuckers had begun to make themselves known on land again. Whether they had escaped from Atlantis or just never left with it, she wasn't sure. The werewolves and Aristotle Society had come together quickly in those times to force the vampires to hide from the humans.

When the werewolves saw that the vampires were mostly under control, they had cut off the relationship. That's when the Aristotle Society enlisted the help of witches and created these tools to hold the werewolves captive and themselves in a position of power over humans.

It was a dark time, and it led to darker days for werewolves like herself; trapped and forced into servitude.

"Sniff it out," Brandon demanded.

Lilly took in the night air, she could taste it, the hint of stolen blood and something else, something evil. There was a monster in the city far worse than a vampire.

Sticking to shadows and trying to make her body look small when anyone was near, they made their way around the city. She couldn't get a clear trail on a vampire, there was more than one here and they had been throughout the city many times. How had Brandon just now figured out that there were vampires in the city? Some of the trails she smelled were a month or more old. She lost even more respect for the man with that realization.

Lilly ignored the smell of the other monster and focused on the bloodsuckers. Eventually she found a trail that seemed fresh, and she followed it with determination to an alley.

When she spotted him there, she couldn't hold back a low growl that alerted him to her presence. Even after all this time her instincts were kicking in, she wanted to rip this dangerous beast apart. No one should prey upon humans, even dumb ones like Brandon.

The vampire dropped what he'd been holding and crouched. Sword in hand he faced down the alley toward them. Behind her she felt Brandon stiffen, felt his movements as he fumbled with something at his belt, probably a gun. She smelled Brandon's fear as they faced the enemy together and knew the vampire would smell it too.

I am going to die here because of this idiot, she thought.

"You mean to challenge me?" the vampire asked in a low tone.

Brandon walked forward with a confidence that she was sure came from her presence. He wouldn't turn and run as long as she was there to protect him. "I am Brandon of the Aristotle Society," Brandon said with a shaky voice.

"Where is your army?" the vampire demanded.

"I don't need an army against one bloodsucker."

Lilly had no way to tell him that this vampire wasn't alone in the city. The assumption that he was, would likely be Brandon's downfall. She couldn't let that happen. Her ears were perked to all sounds around them, she was drawing in the air, constantly assessing for a change, for the approach of any others. She refused to die here, a prisoner of this man, or any man. Fresh air and a perspective on the changing world had given her a renewed determination to get away, to survive. Brandon would make a mistake someday, and she would be ready to take advantage.

"What, no wooden stake?" the vampire laughed.

"I'm told a wooden bullet will do," Brandon said with less confidence.

The vampire frowned and Lilly was interested to hear that it wasn't silver bullets he'd been threatening her with all these years but wood. They would hurt a lot less than silver; she'd have to remember that in case she ever saw freedom on the other side of his raised gun.

She assumed the bullets would kill this monster though, if hit correctly. As would her teeth, given the chance to rip into him deep enough to bleed him out. Why wasn't Brandon letting her do her job? She needed off the leash.

She could feel Brandon shake slightly behind her and she doubted the bloodsucker was taking him seriously. She watched him though, threatening him with her snarl. She would protect the idiot behind her, and happily rip out this vampire's throat if he got close enough.

The vampire's face broke into a wicked smile. "Where is your sire, who is your teacher?"

Brandon shook more and Lilly growled. This vampire could see through Brandon so easily, knew that this was an untrained, untried, and incapable enemy. But she wasn't, and she growled to assure the vampire that she knew exactly how to handle him.

The vampire took a step forward. "Are you all alone? I've faced armies of your ancestors and yet I am still here. You think to take me down alone and obviously untrained, with a malnourished werewolf and a wooden bullet?"

"Others are on their way to the city," Brandon said with false confidence.

The vampire took another step and Brandon stepped back, forcing Lilly to step back as well. She hated that it made her seem weak.

"Brave of you to come out hunting before they arrive," the vampire hissed.

"Stay back! I'll release her!" Brandon's voice shook.

The vampire's eyes assessed Lilly and she felt ashamed to know he found her lacking as an opponent. She wasn't strong, wasn't healthy; but she was determined to live. She would fight to her last to live.

"You are alone, untrained, and that beast you have on the chain is as likely to turn and rip out your throat as mine if you let her loose," the vampire laughed darkly. "I think you know that. I don't think you'll let her go."

A new wash of fear wafted off Brandon and he pulled the trigger. Bullets were fast, but not fast enough. The bullet did hit the vampire, she could smell the blood, but he didn't go down, so she knew it wasn't a kill shot. Lilly was ready to capitalize on the moment but Brandon couldn't keep his feet under him and fell.

He needed to let her do her job, why wasn't he letting her do her job?

Lilly watched the vampire disappear into the building and knew she wouldn't be able to get to him now, not even if Brandon let her off the leash. She could try and alert him to where the vampire had gone, but why? He had no idea how to work a hunt and they'd just lost a lone vampire because of it. The sun rose, its rays licking along the side of the building and a moment of satisfaction hit Lilly as she smelled the burn of vampire flesh. He hadn't quite made it into safety, though she was sure he was very much still alive and well.

"Stupid bitch, you let him go," Brandon snapped at her.

She growled and stared at him unblinking. He was blaming her for this?

He stood up and dusted the dirt from his clothes, then yanked her chain. "Next time you pull me over like that you'll be sorry," he muttered, but she could tell there was a new caution to his words. He needed to stop underestimating her. If she became just a bit more suicidal, she'd tear out his throat and end this torture for the both of them.

Four

HE DIDN'T SPEAK to her until she was back in the cage. With the bars between them his confidence was higher once again. He threw the bolt on the cage. "Stupid bitch," he sneered. "You let him get away, what the hell are you even good for?"

She just looked at him, she didn't need to snarl to intimidate him.

Brandon kicked the bars of the cage. "Next time, you'd better cooperate, or you won't be seeing any meat for a week," he threatened.

She laid down, her head on her paws and stared at him. She could tell it unnerved him, he wanted to be in charge, wanted to think she was his pet. She wasn't, and her calm demeanor, her refusal to cower from him, proved that.

He moved closer to the cage, and she wondered if he was going to open it, to try and prove his dominance. She hoped he did, hoped he was dumb enough to take her collar off, too. She'd kill him so quick he wouldn't even have time to realize his mistake.

"You down there, cuz?" Glen's voice drifted down the stairwell, stopping Brandon with his hand on the latch.

Brandon turned from the cage. "Yeah! Coming up," he called back.

She moved at his turned back, silent, and swift. He shivered and turned slowly back to the cage.

She stood with teeth bared, letting her hatred show in her eyes.

"Christ," he said on a breath and stumbled up the stairs.

Lilly settled down. He hadn't put the chains back on her and she licked at her healing wounds. Another day or two without the silver chains and the skin would be completely closed over. Then another couple of days and the hair would be regrown. She would be looking okay within a week and if she came across another werewolf, they wouldn't look at her with pity, she hoped.

She tried not to think about the fact that there had been something very obviously missing from the scents in the city.

Not a single werewolf. Nowhere they'd gone had she even gotten a hint of one. The realization was terrifying.

It would explain why there were scents from possibly five or six different vampires in the city though. No werewolves around to drive them out. Werewolves would never share their territory with a vampire. It wouldn't explain why Brandon hadn't known about the vampires in the city, however. What had suddenly changed? What had tipped him off? She knew the trails weren't all old, which meant the vamps had been and still were, active in the city. So why did Brandon just now know about them?

She remembered that other scent, the monster, the deep evil. What the hell was that? Was it why there were no werewolves? Or did it have something to do with why Brandon suddenly knew that vampires were running around his city unchecked?

Was she alone in more than just this city?

Was she the last werewolf?

She'd watched plenty of werewolves die of sickness since she'd been captured, was it possible that whatever that had been, had also affected the werewolves everywhere?

She shook with emotion as she felt the loneliness fill her. She'd held out hope that someday, someone would rescue her. But what if there was no one? What if there were only monsters? She whined and tucked her nose to her tail. She closed her eyes and tried to sleep, hoping for dreams of running through fields with her pack, chasing rabbits.

Days passed and Lilly mostly saw Glen. He came every day to feed her which was unusual enough, but he was also bringing her good fresh meat each time instead of the frozen shit she was used to. Her body was starting to heal faster with it, and she could feel her strength renewing. The next time Brandon took her out into the city to hunt a vampire she'd be more confident in her ability to take it down.

She wasn't anxious to come across whatever other monster was out there though, its unfamiliar smell still pinged around in her brain, unable to place it. She knew instinctively that it was bad. What if the vampires had decided to work with the monsters? That was a terrifying thought.

When Brandon walked down the stairs a few days later she was sitting up, looking at him expectantly. She'd heard their exuberant conversation upstairs, tonight they would hunt vampires.

"Dumb bitch animal," Brandon sneered and picked up the leash. "Time to do your job and hunt down some bloodsuckers."

She gave a silent snarl. He used his words to cover his fear, he had no idea how much she could tell by the stench coming from him. She let him attach the leash without complaint. She wanted out, even if it was just a short hunting trip.

"Good bitch," he said.

Glen rushed down the stairs with a wide smile that showed at least one missing tooth. The man looked more idiotic than Brandon and that was saying a lot. Dirty tank top and shorts made from an old pair of jeans was what he thought was a great idea for hunting vampires. At least he wore boots, though they were untied... he did have weapons strapped to his body though, so that was something.

Brandon was dressed slightly better in a leather jacket that looked old and worn. He too wore shorts, which she had to admit were weather-appropriate, but not hunting attire. His boots were tied, so maybe he'd be able to stay on his feet better this time and his belt seemed to have been adjusted to fit.

Maybe they'd survive the night.

She couldn't believe these two were her masters. It would be laughable if it wasn't such a depressing and harsh reality.

And since it was her reality and all she could hope for at the moment was a taste of controlled freedom, she went eagerly with them, up the stairs and through the store.

As soon as they were outside, she smelled it. Not vampires, not a monster, werewolves! She pulled at the leash, anxious to get to them, desperate for help. There were three of them, she could smell each individual and one was an alpha, his scent prickled different in her brain, warning her to be cautious. They weren't her pack, this wasn't her alpha, but she didn't care what pack they were from. All that she cared about was that they were here in the city, and this might be her only chance to alert them to her existence, to get help.

Brandon and Glen couldn't smell what she did, so they went along with excitement, thinking they were about to bag a vampire. Hopefully they wouldn't realize anything was off until it was too late.

She pulled on her leash and tried to run, but Brandon wouldn't let her, and her heart ached. Her mind kept racing around the fact that she wasn't alone in this world. The realization made her all the more desperate to stay alive, to find a way to get out of Brandon's control. Maybe they'd recognize her, just because she didn't recognize their scents didn't mean they'd never met before. Or perhaps her father had spread the word of his missing daughter. His all black, werewolf daughter, and they'd know and even if they couldn't save her tonight, they'd alert her father and he would burn down the city to save her, she knew he would.

She knew how dangerous to her mental state hope could be, how crushing the disappointment would be if she was mistaken, or if she couldn't find them. None of that mattered now though. She'd deal with depression after, if it came to that. Right now she was floating on a high of possibilities. Nothing could be worse than not finding them, except, what if Brandon and Glen captured them too? That thought nearly stopped her in her tracks. Was she leading doom to these other werewolves?

No, she was certain Brandon and Glen weren't smart enough, weren't prepared enough, to capture any werewolves. It had taken five armed men and a well sprung trap to capture her.

She pushed on toward hope, practically dragging Brandon behind her. Glen was complaining about how heavy the bag he lugged along was.

"Told you we don't need all that shit," Brandon said.

"That's not what your pa said, this is the stuff that was on the list for going out on a hunt," Glen defended with a huff.

"Then carry it and shut up," Brandon said.

Glen grunted and wheezed as he tried to keep up. "The museum?" Glen questioned as they stopped outside of a large dark building.

She wanted to jump forward, she knew they were there, right inside, but Brandon had stopped and Glen was leaning on his knees beside them trying to catch his breath. He pulled out a cigarette and lit it, dropping the heavy bag on the ground.

"There was a break-in and murder here recently," Brandon said. "Maybe it was a vamp attack and he came back for more?"

"Maybe she's just smelling an old trail," Glen countered, motioning with his lit cigarette.

"Only one way to find out. Get it," Brandon said and started forward.

Lilly could smell their scent strongly, the werewolves were just inside, she was so close. She pulled harder, desperate to get in there. Brandon walked with her to the doorway, Glen close behind.

She growled as she stood in the open doorway, wanting to scream to be released from Brandon's control.

She could hardly believe her eyes; three werewolf men stood in the warehouse.

It didn't matter that they weren't in wolf form, she would recognize them anywhere. Big strong males, they could surely help her. Her eyes skipped over the small human that was with them, she didn't matter, all that mattered was this chance at freedom.

The group turned with looks of surprise. She heard them gasp. "What the fuck is that?" one of the males said.

"A female, how the fuck do you have a female?" another growled. This was the alpha she'd scented and he was close to shifting, she could hear it in his voice. Her eyes were locked with another, a werewolf that hadn't spoken. He stared at her with lust and desire, and it burned through her like a caress. She knew that look well, had seen it plenty of times in her life and they'd all ended in heartache.

"She's tracking a vamp, where is the bloodsucker?" Brandon demanded.

"No, she's tracking an alpha. She looks half dead," the alpha snarled, looking at her with fury.

Lilly growled, feeling slightly threatened because she wasn't part of his pack, it wasn't safe to wander into another pack's territory, and her instincts were to run, hide, or fight even as she desperately wanted them to save her.

The alpha's body started to ripple and the small human stepped away from him, afraid. Smart girl, werewolves often hurt those around them unintentionally.

The three werewolf men stepped toward her and Brandon pulled back on the chain, making her yip. The werewolves froze.

"Take another step and I'll shoot," Brandon threatened. "Where's the vamp?"

"No vamps here, boy, who the hell are you?" the alpha demanded.

"Brandon, leader of the Aristotle Society and handler of this weapon," he yanked the chain again. "This is my cousin, Glen."

"Aristotle Society!" another gasped. "I thought you were gone."

"Not gone and not interested in lies. I don't give a shit about you wolves; we hunt vamps, and she led us here so what the hell is *she*?" Brandon pointed his gun at the woman, and she took a step back.

"Human," she said quickly, holding up her hands.

"I want one," Glen said from behind Brandon, no doubt meaning the werewolf men. This is what she'd feared but she had to believe that Brandon and Glen didn't have what was necessary to capture one, let alone, three, werewolves.

"Idiot," the human hissed.

"Where's the vamp then?" Brandon demanded.

"She might just smell the vampire scent on me," the woman explained quickly.

"A vampire whore?" Brandon sneered and raised his gun. "A good enough reason for me."

Brandon shot at the woman, one werewolf jumped to push her out of the way and the alpha lunged for Brandon and Glen.

Lilly reacted instinctively, she had to protect Brandon. The man who hadn't yet spoken, shifted to a beautiful red wolf with bright blue eyes and gleaming white teeth. He leaped toward Brandon's group. He was bigger than her and easily leaped right over her to get to Brandon who swung his gun around too late. Brandon cried out as the wolf's jaws bit down on his hand. Lilly leaped at the wolf, she couldn't allow him to kill Brandon, not while he wore the ring. She easily pushed the wolf off Brandon. They rolled and snarled at each other but he submitted quickly.

She looked up at Brandon, he was holding his arm, his gun

hand mangled. The stench of his blood was pungent, and her mouth watered slightly.

Glen was gone, that didn't surprise her; coward.

"She'll tear his throat out if you so much as move," Brandon said to the other wolves.

Lilly could smell the other wolf's blood too, he'd been wounded by Brandon's gun, but he wasn't dead, she could hear his heart still beating. She was thankful for that; she didn't want to risk the alpha blaming her for the death of one of his packmates.

Glen stepped back into the room, surprising Lilly. He must have gone back out for whatever was in the bag he'd left outside. He held a gun up.

"What do you want?" the alpha growled.

"We won't kill that bitch, for now. But we're keeping this wolf." He motioned to the werewolf staring up at her. "These two can breed us some nice pups, can't they, Glen?"

"Sure as shit!" Glen said and spat on the floor.

They still don't know, Lilly thought. *Same mistake, different idiots*. She looked into the wolf's eyes and wondered if he knew. Was she still the only female? They'd reacted to her presence as if shocked that she existed, so she guessed she was.

"I suggest you start making new friends if you want to keep breathing, I won't hesitate to kill you next time I come around and you're smelling like you've been with a bloodsucker," Brandon threatened the woman.

The alpha shifted into a large black wolf and stood in front of the woman with bared fangs. It didn't surprise Lilly to see a werewolf defend a human, but a human who admittedly took blood from a vampire, that was a surprise. What had changed in the years she'd been in that cage?

"Shit, he's huge," Glen said, taking a step back, his gun trembling.

Coward, Lilly thought.

"Just get a collar on this male," Brandon ordered, "I need to get stitched." He was darting glances at the wolf he'd shot. Lilly wondered if he was finally realizing how dangerous a wolf without one of these collars could be.

Glen moved nearer to the male. The male didn't try to escape, he just looked at her with eyes full of hope and desire and Lilly wasn't sure that was a good thing. What if he didn't know trying to breed was hopeless? She didn't really want to go through all of that again.

Glen easily slipped the collar around the male's neck, but Lilly noticed there was no ring going around either man's finger. Did they not have one, or did they not realize it was necessary?

Soon they were backing out of the building and the male watched her with an intensity that made her shiver.

"Be safe brother," the alpha whispered as they left, having shifted back to human.

"Holy shit, man, I can't believe we got another one," Glen said as they moved quickly away from the building.

Lilly darted her gaze to the male, his ears were alert for danger, his eyes scanned their surroundings, and she could tell he was scenting the air continuously. He was working to protect her, and that knowledge warmed something in her.

"I'm going to kick its ass for biting me," Brandon whispered.

Lilly wished she could smile. The scent of Brandon's blood in the air pleased her. She would have liked to see him bleed out on the floor completely. Of course, not while he wore the ring.

She continued to watch the male as they went, she hated that she couldn't communicate with him like this, except in the most basic ways. She wondered what he knew about their situation; if he understood how it worked. She especially wanted to be sure he wouldn't accidentally kill Brandon, and her. She wanted him to know that she wasn't with them by choice. If he had a chance to get them away, she'd go too.

She wished she could ask if he knew her father, if he knew of the Georgia pack. There had been no recognition in the eyes of any of the wolves when they'd seen her and that worried her. Either her father hadn't sent the world out looking for her, had given up on finding her, or her father was gone.

That thought threatened to break her. She stumbled a step, and the male was immediately at her side, his head rubbed against her in a gentle question. She bumped back in reassurance; she was fine to keep going.

"Look at that, they're friendly," Glen said.

Brandon grunted.

Five

BRANDON DIRECTED her back through the city to a parking lot behind the shop. Relief washed through her at not being taken back inside and to the cage. The longer she was outside of it, the greater her chances for escape or alerting her father, and now with the male beside her, she was filled with more hope than she'd had in so many years.

"There," Brandon ordered and waved a hand at a white van. "Put them inside," he told Glen and threw her leash to him before walking to the passenger side door.

"Okay lovebirds," Glen said as he opened the back door of the van. "Don't mess anything up and stay out of the bait box."

Lilly hesitated, looking into the small space packed with things she didn't understand. The smell of rotting fish was strong, and she really didn't want to go in there.

"Up, girl," Glen urged, and the male werewolf growled. "You too, big boy."

"What the hell is going on back there, I'm bleeding to death," Brandon yelled from the front.

"Up," Glen said again, this time he poked her with the gun.

Lilly looked from the van to the male werewolf then jumped

34

in. It was better than the cell. He followed right behind her, putting himself between her and Glen protectively.

The door shut but no lock sounded, it would be so easy to break out. One mistake after another with these men. If only busting out of the back of the van and running away would solve her problems.

The male looked at her questioningly and she sat to show that she wanted to stay put for now. He whined a bit but sat as well, looking at her with a million questions in his eyes.

"Do you really think they'll do it?" Glen asked.

"If they don't want to, we make them," Brandon said with a laugh. "Fuck, this hurts. Give me something, what do you have stashed in here?"

Lilly couldn't help the whine at those words, so familiar, so full of painful memories. The male growled and Brandon hit the bars that separated them with his good hand and laughed again. "Don't act like you won't enjoy it, you little bitch."

Glen laughed as he started to drive out of the parking lot. "Check the glovebox, might be a few pills in there. Why didn't they come after their friend?" he wondered out loud.

"Dumb dogs probably don't have any loyalty to each other, and besides, they could tell who was in control! No one messes with the men of the Aristotle Society." Brandon was silent for a moment. "I hope your sister is home and can take care of this hand."

"Yeah, she doesn't strip on Wednesdays, so she should be."

Lilly stopped listening to the two up front and looked at the male, wishing she could speak to him, wishing she could know his name at the very least. It was embarrassing to be in an intimate situation with a male and not even know their name. He laid down and stared up at her submissively, signaling his willingness to concede to her judgment of their situation. She stepped to him and did the only thing she could think to do in that moment. She started to bathe him softly, it really was in their best interest to like each other.

"Oh good, she likes him," Brandon said.

The male's eyes lifted and looked at Brandon. Lilly was happy to see Brandon shudder and quickly look away. She cuddled up to the male, enjoying the feeling of protection. Her instincts told her that he would protect her, no words necessary to understand the possessiveness in his eyes. It would frighten her if she wasn't already owned by two idiotic humans.

"I think I've lost too much blood," Brandon said.

Lilly's body shifted as Glen took a corner faster than was probably safe. Luckily it just put her closer to the male who had barely budged despite the rocking of the van.

Lilly looked at the male who seemed to remain alert even as he laid on the floor. Why hadn't he fought the collar? Did he know something she didn't? She had to hope he had some kind of plan. At least there were others out there now that knew about her. Certainly his pack would be coming for him, would they save her too?

Real hope like she hadn't known in years filled her as she breathed in the scent of another werewolf. She didn't have to pretend she wasn't alone as her eyes slid shut. She drifted to sleep quickly, lulled by the calmer movements of the van as well as the presence of the wolf. She hated to admit it, but her body was tired from the exercise and excitement of the evening.

She dreamed of passion. A tall stranger with no clear face but his body was warm and muscled, his hands rough as they moved across her skin. One hand moved from her naked belly up between her breasts to rest gently around her throat. He leaned in and kissed her, nipping at her lower lip then sliding his tongue into her mouth. He tasted like honey.

He artfully worked the kiss, his hand never leaving her neck, it grounded her, not letting the passion take her away no matter how desperately she wanted it to. She felt her body heat, to tremble and burn but she couldn't get there, couldn't find that perfect release because of the hand.

Then it wasn't a hand, it was a collar and Brandon's face leered down at her as she cried and shivered. Naked and afraid at the feet of a man who had caused her so much pain. The strong stranger was gone but she could still smell him, could still taste him in her mouth.

But she was alone. It was just her and Brandon and there was no hope of anything else for her, not ever.

* * *

Tray breathed in the scent of the werewolf sleeping next to him. She whined in her sleep and twitched. He wished he could soothe her bad dreams, wished he could replace them with anything her heart desired. His tail twitched in irritation at their situation. Two men of the Aristotle Society were nothing against his claws and teeth.

If it were just him and them, he'd be out of this van in minutes, and they'd be dead. He looked down at her and watched her leg twitch as if she were running in her sleep. It wasn't just him though, and hopefully it never would be again.

Tray was consumed by his need to be with her. The moment he saw her nothing else existed, only her. He had been desperate to free her when he'd leapt at Brandon, but she'd defended the human. His world threatened to crash around him in that moment as thoughts had filled his mind. Was she with the human? Was this horrible man her lover? The idea of tearing the human apart held more appeal in that instant than before, nothing would keep Tray from having her, he could feel in his soul that she was meant to be his. Certainly she'd realize it too once the obstacle was removed.

That's when he'd seen the ring, and he knew in his gut that the stories were true, the Aristotle Society held a power that bound their life to the wolf's.

Not her lover, her captor.

If he killed Brandon, she would die too. It gave him hope though, so he submitted to her and waited as they'd clamped a collar around his neck. An eternity of servitude by her side was better than a free moment without her.

The cinch of the silver around his neck had been like a slap in the face. His shifting ability was taken from him, and he'd had to force himself not to freak out. He looked into her deep gold eyes and saw his future there, it grounded him. Already there was nothing without her, he would endure anything for her.

Tray curled himself around her small form as best he could as the van bumped along the road. She was so small, so underfed, and her fur was patchy in places. He wondered if she'd been held with silver recently, not much else could leave those kinds of slowly healing wounds. He wanted to rip through both men for treating her like this. She trembled against him in her sleep.

The van rocked to a stop, and he jumped up, standing over her protectively. She jerked awake, sitting up next to him, and staring at the back door. He couldn't decide what to do if they opened it, he knew he couldn't attack Brandon, but he could kill Glen. Of course if he got himself shot for it, then what was the point? He needed to wait, they were idiots, they'd make a mistake, and he would capitalize on it. They'd already made one very big mistake; they hadn't linked his life to either of them. Was it coming, or did they not realize each collar needed its own ring? He had a feeling they didn't know a lot.

The front doors of the van opened and closed, then voices drifted away. They weren't being taken out apparently, so he relaxed a bit. Tray looked at her and whined. He hated that he couldn't communicate with her, didn't know her name or anything about her.

But other than the fact that she was his, what else mattered right now? They had a lifetime to get to know each other.

She looked at him unsure. Was she frightened of him? Did she expect him to harm her just because he was stronger? The thought that she might have been mistreated by other males in the past made him see red, but he swallowed it back because he had no way to release it, no one to target. Right now he needed to make sure she knew that she was safe with him. That was the most important thing.

He sat and cocked his head to the side. She mimicked him, cocking her head to the side. It was adorable and made his heart ache all the more for her. He lifted up a paw and she mimicked him again. They touched paws as if high fiving and if he could have smiled, he would have. He settled for letting his tongue dangle from his mouth in a goofy wolfy grin.

She dropped her paw and walked closer, putting her head under his in a protective stance. She was telling him that she would watch out for him. She was emaciated, but so fierce. She must have been through hell and for longer than he cared to imagine, but she was strong in spirit, and she was all his.

Tray's chest rumbled approval and he licked from her head down to her neck, stopping at the offending collar. His teeth scraped against it, but the silver made him shiver and pull back.

She yipped, agreeing with his assessment. There was no taking them off without human hands. He laid down and she settled against him with a heavy sigh. Whatever they were going to face with these men, they would face it together.

Breeding.

The word ran through Tray's mind. Brandon and Glen wanted werewolf pups. Tray didn't think it was possible. He'd never heard of a breeding pair of werewolves. The rumors of females were few and far between and never included pups. What kind of torturous life would be in store for his children if it was possible? Too horrifying to consider.

He settled in to think. Obviously, the men didn't know how to properly care for a wolf, she was in rough shape. They didn't know how to recognize a vampire on sight either because they hadn't been sure that Katherine wasn't one. They had the equipment, or at least part of it, to be Aristotle Society members even if they didn't know how to use it properly. So they had likely inherited her and the supplies unexpectedly, without proper training on how to do the job. Brandon's father perhaps, died suddenly and still young. It would explain a lot.

The Aristotle Society was thought to be extinct. It seemed lately a lot of things were coming back into play that never should have been seen again. First the monster from Atlantis, a foul beast that had been imprisoned with so many others in the city before it had sunk. Thanks to the vampire king's brother, it was released into Miami to help him get a stone to use against the Descendants of Atlantis, that poor unfortunate race of humans that were once blood slaves to the vampires. Now this. It was as if the fates had decided life was too easy and it was time to shake things up.

There was nothing supernaturally powerful about the Aristotle Society members, which meant that there was nothing keeping Brandon and Glen from trying to recruit more members. It was difficult to turn a human into a werewolf or vampire and monsters were something else altogether, a mistake of the gods perhaps. But idiots like Brandon, they were a dime a dozen and their ideas spread like a disease among humans. It would be so easy to turn a population into werewolf-trapping vampire-hunters with a complete disregard to the consequences of the balance of nature and the individual. Because as much as Tray hated to admit it, he knew that vampires were not all bloodthirsty monsters.

He'd recently witnessed two vampires who were each enamored and protective of a human in a way that indicated a deep love. No monster could be capable of what he'd seen between Ian and Katherine. Or feel what Samson obviously felt for the Descendant Sorcha.

There was no drive to love or protect in these Aristotle men or their ancestors, never had been. The Society's desire to kill vampires had started as a play for power, a reveling in what the witches had gifted them with and passed down in generations to where he doubted Brandon and Glen even knew that their tools had come from a powerful witch, the sister to the witch who had created Atlantis actually. But with power came a price. For the Aristotle Society it had been a sort of madness, a power-hungry desire to obtain, kill, and glory in their own righteousness.

The power of being a werewolf came with a hefty price too, a lonely price. He may have hated it more than not in his long lifetime, but now that he'd seen Lilly he'd live a hundred lifetimes of torment and loneliness to be with her here and now. He needed to find a way to get them both to safety so that they could begin their life together, both of them deserved it.

His mind swirled around the facts he knew and how he might use them to get her out of this mess. He came up blank. Their only hope might be waiting for his packmates he'd left behind at the museum, Patrick and Dallas. He knew they wouldn't abandon him, but Dallas was injured, and Patrick wouldn't give up on his search for the Blood Moonstone so easily either. It was going to change everything for the werewolves. A powerful stone that could prevent a werewolf from shifting with the moon.

All that meant saving them would be third on their list. He understood it, but it didn't sit well when he looked over at the female and desperately wanted to know her name and what she looked like as a human and every detail about her life up until now.

Did she realize that she was his everything now? Could she feel the connection like he did?

She whined and laid down, avoiding his eyes.

Did she see the intensity in his gaze and shy away from it?

He tried to calm his mind, tried to soften the need in his eyes and began to softly bathe her face.

She tucked her tail and backed away.

Damnit, he'd scared her, and he hadn't even told her what he was thinking. He turned from her and sat facing the back door. He was giving her as much space as he could, more than he'd like to.

He couldn't stand the thought of her being afraid of him though, he'd do anything to prevent that.

He couldn't stand the thought of being a monster in her eyes.

* * *

Brandon cursed and drank heavily from a jar as Rylee worked on his hand. "Are you sure you know what you're doing?" he asked.

"I'm going to nursin' school when I'm not dancin'. I know stuff, and shit, this is bad," Rylee said.

"You mean you took an online first aid course," Glen laughed from the kitchen where he made himself a sandwich and chugged a beer, a lit cigarette hung from his lips.

"Shut up!" Rylee snapped and threw a bloody rag at Glen. "I'm signed up for a class starting next week. I'm gonna be a real nurse and not just the sexy kind." She waggled her eyebrows at Brandon.

Glen laughed from the kitchen and Brandon took another swig from the jar of moonshine. His eyes drifted up and down Rylee. She was cute, big tits and a slim waist, but she had no ass and he'd always appreciated a girl with more curves than less. Her face was alright, until she smiled. Teeth rotten from drugs he knew for a fact she hadn't given up. She'd hit him up for a loan just last week because she was itching for a fix.

Her being his cousin was lowest on the list of reasons he wouldn't take her for a tumble in the sack and with each swig that list got smaller and smaller.

"Done." She sat back and grabbed the jar from him, taking a long swig.

Brandon lifted his hand and stared at the bandages, already soaking through with blood. "I think I need a real medic."

"Well fuck you! I did what I could. Dog bites are nasty, you probably have rabies."

"Glen, drive me to the clinic."

"Sure and what do you plan to do with the *dogs* while you're in getting stitched up? If they make noise back there someone could call it in, people get bent out of shape about dogs in cars," Glen said as he bit into a sandwich and then smiled, showing a gross amount of food in his teeth.

Brandon looked at Rylee and lifted an eyebrow in question.

"I'll take you," she said with a sigh. "I'm not dog-sitting any beast that did that to your hand. I can't afford to miss a day of work, and tips when you're bleeding are not as good as you'd expect." She got up and grabbed her purse, slipping into a pair of flip flops. She walked out of the house and Brandon stood to follow.

"Toss me that rag, I don't want to bleed all over the car."

Glen tossed it to him and grinned. "Have fun."

"Don't let them out while I'm gone." He handed Glen the ring. "Wear that, they won't attack you if you're wearing that."

"Why?" Glen asked, looking down at the silver band.

It had some kind of inscription that Brandon couldn't read. He shrugged, he didn't know why or how it worked, but his father had told him that he had to always wear it when dealing with the bitch. It would protect him. So far it always had, so he supposed it worked. Probably some kind of voodoo magic, he wasn't sure he believed in that shit but then again once you saw a man shift into a wolf, you were willing to believe almost anything. His father had died unexpectedly at the end of a gun outside the shop. He hadn't had a chance to tell Brandon everything and up until that point Brandon hadn't been too interested in the caged wolf under the shop. He'd never even seen his father or uncle take her out and it had felt like a burden more than anything to keep her. Now though, now it made him feel powerful and he liked it. He wanted to sic her on a vamp, see her tear it apart and beg for mercy at Brandon's feet. He couldn't wait to take the big guy out hunting, too. Man would he get laid hard after showing a chick what he could protect her from.

Brandon adjusted his crotch.

Glen spun the thing around his pinky. "Like some kind of superhero shit? Is it going to give me superpowers?"

"Just wear it," Brandon snapped. He flexed his hand, feeling odd without the ring. His head started to spin from the blood loss. He stumbled out of the house and into Rylee's car.

"You don't look so good," Rylee said as he closed his eyes and put his head back against the seat.

"Just drive."

"If you die in my car, I'm feeding you to the gators out at Stan's place," she warned as she sped down the driveway and out onto the main road.

They were a good twenty minutes from town and then another ten from the clinic. He hoped he would make it.

"If my brother finds my stash, I'll feed you to the gators too," Rylee added.

Brandon grunted and turned his head to look at her through half-open eyes. "Glen can smell that shit a mile away, might as well assume it's gone."

"Family sucks."

"Don't worry, maybe you can give the doctors at the ER a lap dance for extra cash."

She shifted in her seat slightly and stuck her fingers under the crotch of her short cutoffs. "No underwear so I could probably make that work," she said with a grin and pulled her hand back up, slapping it onto the steering wheel.

"You're disgusting," Brandon said and closed his eyes again.

Rylee just laughed and turned the radio up, blasting Britney Spears.

Six

LILLY WAS STARING at the male's back, trying to decide how she felt about his intensity when she heard a car driving off. She wondered if they'd been left alone here and if that even mattered. There was a new relief in her body that told her either Brandon's bleeding had stopped, or he'd taken the ring off.

She moved to stand next to the male, trying not to think too much about what was going to happen next to either one of them. He smelled so good, and she was almost embarrassed by the way she was desperately breathing him in. She didn't want to ever forget his smell, or the feel of his warm, breathing body beside hers. If she spent the next month right there in the back of that van next to him, she would be happy. Werewolves weren't meant to live alone; they needed a pack.

Both their ears perked as the crunch of footsteps sounded outside and came closer. She felt him tense up beside her. The back door of the van opened, and Glen stood there with a stupid grin, a cigarette hanging from his lips, and a glassy look to his eyes. He smelled terrible, like poison and she wrinkled her nose in protest. Beside her the male sneezed, equally put off by Glen's scent. But as she looked at Glen, she recognized a connection there, he was wearing the ring now. Did that mean Brandon was dead? Or had he just not trusted that they wouldn't kill Glen while he was gone unless Glen had the ring? Maybe Brandon was smarter than she'd given him credit for.

Probably not.

"Well, how about some food?" Glen said far too brightly to be considered normal. "My sister doesn't have much in the kitchen for dogs, but you're wild animals so why not let you go catch something in the woods? There's got to be some possum out there or maybe the neighbor has got a cat. Do you eat snake?"

Lilly put her ears back, mistrusting what she was hearing.

Beside her the male wolf's chest rumbled, untrusting as well. He stepped forward and Glen stepped back, leaving space for them to jump out. The male did and his head whipped around, searching for danger, maybe expecting a trap. He looked back at her and silently indicated that it all looked safe. Lilly hopped out; gaze locked on Glen. She didn't trust this. They were both still wearing leashes, but Glen made no move to grab them and control where they could go.

"I don't think you guys are as dangerous as all that, I think you understand me and know that if you try to run off, I'll hunt you down." He waved a gun around for emphasis. Whether it had bullets to kill a vampire or a werewolf she couldn't be sure, but either way, she wasn't interested in finding out. "So, go on, get a meal and then come back and get in the mood for baby making, I have plans for those pups."

Glen removed their leashes and threw them into the back of the van.

Lilly looked at the male and he twitched his tail then darted his eyes to the dark woods. She took off in the direction he'd indicated, and he followed. Unbelievably, Glen didn't follow or shout for them to come back, or shoot at them. Was this a dream?

She ran uninhibited and the male followed. She circled trees, jumped over rocks, and felt her feet push into dirt. A million wonderful smells filled her with knowledge of all the things that were near and all the choices she had. She could run or she could dig, chase or howl. She had more freedom than she'd had in so long. She wanted to cry with the joy of it and cry at the certainty that she would have to return to Glen.

The collar hung heavy on her neck, a reminder that she wasn't really free. She couldn't just not go back; it was too risky. She didn't know what would happen if she tried to remove the collar while Glen wore the ring. She didn't know if the spell was set so that such a thing would kill her. The witches were powerful and vindictive. They could have woven any number of traps into the spell. She had a sense of where the ring was, so she had to assume the ring wearer would have a sense of where the collar was too. If she tried to run still wearing it, she'd be easily tracked. One thing she was pretty sure of, both Glen and Brandon knew how to track and hunt.

All this freedom she felt at her fingertips was temporary at best.

She pushed through the crushing reality, deciding on physical exertion over emotion and it wasn't long before she reached a small stream. She lapped at the fresh water happily before jumping in. The feel of cold water rushing around her body was euphoric and for a few minutes she just rolled and floated and felt years of dust and dead skin flow from her body. An alligator floated nearby watching cautiously but it could sense the danger that she was. She was the apex predator here and it wouldn't approach her unless she threatened it directly.

The male sat on the side of the creek as if he were on guard duty. He watched her and the surroundings, making her feel safe. With him acting as sentry she forgot the world for a few glorious moments and just enjoyed the act of swimming. When she stepped out, she shook droplets from her body and howled up at the sky in delight.

He howled with her and somewhere way off in the distance another werewolf answered their call.

The unexpected response frightened her, she crouched and swiveled her ears around searching for sounds of approach. The male immediately stood over her, protecting. He licked her head reassuring, but she wasn't convinced. It had been so long since she'd been outside of that cage, suddenly the world felt too big, and she shivered. What would she do if a pack surrounded her? She was in no condition to fight off a major attack. What if they didn't understand the collar and ring, what if they killed her trying to help her?

Panic filled her, her heart beat so fast she thought she might faint, and a whine escaped her. The male nudged her with his big head, and she knew he was trying to tell her that it was going to be alright, but her body wasn't listening, it was primed to run. The only thing that stopped her was staring into his blue eyes and seeing a plea there that she trust him. He seemed desperate to convey to her that he knew what was going on and that it was safe.

When she nodded slightly, he howled again, and the answer was closer this time. He was calling someone in. She wanted to hide in the van even as she hoped for rescue. What if Brandon and Glen managed to capture more males? What if they tried to force breeding with all of them? What if it was just like it had been before the Aristotle Society had realized she couldn't carry a pregnancy?

She couldn't face that, couldn't survive that again. Her stomach clenched and the river water threatened to come back up. She whined and laid on the ground. The male remained over her in a protective stance, but he couldn't know what she feared, couldn't understand what she'd already been through.

He howled again and this time the answer was so close she could almost smell them. She whined and tucked her tail as first one, then another wolf stepped into sight.

One was huge and black, she recognized him as the alpha she'd seen at the museum, the other was only slightly smaller, he was light brown with a half white face. Was this the one that had been shot? She hoped it was, hoped he had survived.

The alpha shifted to human and stood before them naked and uncaring. Lilly couldn't help a whine and the male before her stepped between her and the man.

"It's alright Tray, we won't harm the female," the alpha said firmly.

Tray, his name was Tray. She liked knowing that. She darted a quick look at him and saw that he was baring his fangs silently at the alpha. It surprised Lilly to see such a display against his alpha, Tray was a strong wolf and that knowledge filled her with a possessive pride she shouldn't feel for someone she'd just met.

The alpha lifted his hands in a show of peace. "Let me try and remove the collars. Are the humans close?"

Tray gave a quick shake of his head to indicate the direction that Glen was. The other wolf hurried off to check.

Tray sat as the alpha approached and looked at the collar. "It's just a normal buckle collar," he mused and touched it. "Oh, packs a punch though, lots of silver," he said with a hiss, shaking his hands. "It hurts in human form, I can't imagine what it's doing to you in wolf form," he mused. "Is it safe to remove? Do you feel it's attachment to a human with a ring on?"

Tray gave his head a shake, indicating he thought it was safe.

The alpha took the thing off Tray quickly, hissing a bit as he did, then dropped the thing to the ground and gave his hand a shake.

Tray shifted to human.

"I'm so glad to see you, Patrick. There might only be Glen back there still. I think a woman who lives there had to take Brandon to get real medical care for his hand. Glen has the ring attached to her collar though." Tray glanced back at her, and his eyes were full of concern. "I don't know what will happen if we take the collar off while he wears it," Tray explained.

Lilly whined agreement, glad his thoughts mirrored hers. She was desperate to have the thing removed, but not so desperate to risk death.

Tray walked over and knelt beside her. She kept her wary gaze on Patrick. Just because Tray trusted him, didn't mean she would just yet. It had been her experience that throwing a female into a mix of male wolves created a new play for power that could destroy old friends.

"She looks terrified," Patrick said gently, not moving any closer, which she appreciated.

"I think she's been with them for a long time," Tray said and reached out to put a hand on Lilly's head.

She appreciated the touch and licked his hand as it stroked down the side of her face.

"She seems to trust you," Patrick pointed out. "You must have made quite an impression already."

"I will do whatever it takes to free her and protect her after that," Tray said.

Patrick nodded and looked at her. "She is something to protect for sure, and no wolf deserves captivity." Patrick's words were full of all the anger her situation deserved.

The other wolf loped back and shifted to human.

"Dallas, what did you see?" Patrick asked.

"One idiot drinking on the porch, gun in his lap and smoking a cigarette. Not a care in the world. I didn't smell anyone else. We can kill him," Dallas proclaimed.

Lilly whined.

"Not while he's wearing the ring," Tray said quickly. "If he dies with that thing on, she'll die too. I've heard enough about the damn Society to know that much, and it can be the only explanation as to why she hasn't killed the bastards already."

Lilly yipped agreement, hating that she couldn't communicate better with them.

"So take the collar off," Dallas said with exasperation. "Then we can kill him and move on. I don't like hanging out in vamp territory." Dallas gave a snort. "Not that they're currently home."

Lilly whined, she didn't know for sure how to free a collared wolf, and neither did they. The magic was strong and messing with it could kill her. Some days she'd say risk killing her to find out, today though... today she wanted to live.

"We need him to take the ring off first, it's the only way to be sure," Tray said.

Patrick nodded agreement. "So how do we do that without getting shot in the process?"

"Or captured," Dallas mumbled.

Tray knelt down and grabbed her face between his hands, they were large for a human and she enjoyed the firm feel of them as he looked into her eyes. He smiled and it lit up his entire face. "Hey, love. Can you go back? Yip at him, get him worried enough to come looking for me?"

She whined but gave a little nod. Tray stroked her head gently and stood.

"We can catch him off guard and knock him out with a quick punch, then take the ring off," he told the others. "He probably won't come into the trees without the gun though, so watch for it."

She wasn't sure of the plan, it felt flimsy, but she didn't have a better option to offer so she slunk off slow until she was out of sight of the men, then she ran. Her instincts were to stay with them, well with him anyway, Tray. She felt a connection to him, a safety that she didn't want to leave even as his intensity frightened her. But she knew he was right, they had to get the ring off Glen, it was the only way and if they didn't work quickly, they might be too late. They may never have the chance of four against one again.

Would Tray leave with his packmates if this plan failed? The thought almost stopped her. Even if it was temporary, even if he promised to come back later and save her, she knew watching him go and leave her behind still collared to these men would kill her.

This plan couldn't fail. This was her one chance at freedom and she'd sell it because her life depended on it.

Just as Dallas had described, Glen was sitting on the small front porch of the odd-looking rundown home. He was paler than usual, his watery eyes rimmed in red, his lips slightly blue.

"Back already?" Glen slurred as she skidded to a stop in the driveway. "Where's your boyfriend?"

She yipped and ran in a circle. Ran to the edge of the wooded area and back, then yipped again. How did you get an idiot to understand you when you were stuck in wolf form?

"What are you trying to tell me, girl? You been watching Lassie? Did Timmy fall down a well?" Glen laughed at a joke she didn't understand and stood up on wobbly legs. He took a step to follow her, coughed, spewing blood into the wind, then he fell on his face.

She knew the moment his heart stopped, because hers started to as well. This was how it ended, so close to freedom. At least she wouldn't suffer any longer. Maybe word of her would reach her father, if he was alive, maybe he would finally get closure. Her disappearance no longer a mystery. And if he was dead, maybe she was about to be reunited with him in the stars.

Her eyes felt heavy, commotion surrounded her. Tray was there, ripping at the collar on her neck. The others rushed past her, to Glen's body she assumed.

"Get it off of him!" Tray was shouting as the latch of the collar caught and Lilly's body twitched. The world started to go black and in the corner of her vision Lilly saw her, Death shrouded in black was here for her.

The weight of the collar slipped from her neck and Death revealed her face. The white wolf with the red eyes that Lilly had seen the night of her change.

"Not yet," Death whispered and touched Lilly's snout before dissolving into a soft mist.

The touch was an electric shot, and her heart began to pound in her chest once again. She was alive, but she was weak, and she could only close her eyes as her systems rebooted. She felt Tray's presence beside her and took comfort in that as she slipped into healing sleep.

Seven

TRAY GAZED AT her there on the ground, watched her eyes close as he listened desperately to her weak heartbeat. It gave a sudden leap and beat steadier, filling him with hope. She shifted to her human form, and he gasped. She was perfect. Long black hair and dark lashes on a delicate face. Sunken cheeks showed her malnutrition, and her body was so slight, ribs showing clearly and her hip bones jutting out. She looked like he could accidentally snap her if he wasn't careful. He ached with the need to protect and provide for her. There were stripes of scarred skin crossing her torso and back mimicking the marks of thin fur he'd noticed on her wolf form. She must have been held with silver chains for a very long time. He would kill Brandon.

Her skin was so pale it was almost see-through but her nipples were a perfect rosy pink and he wanted to cover her from the eyes of the others. But he didn't even have any clothes on himself.

"Damn," Dallas said, coming up behind him.

Tray glared at the man, growling, and baring his human teeth.

"Don't come near her," Tray ordered.

"We don't have time for that, Tray. We need to get her out of here," Patrick said firmly. "Pick her up, Tray. We parked back that way through the woods."

"Go inside and find a blanket or something," Tray ordered Dallas.

Dallas hurried into the trailer and Tray hoped he would be able to find something decently clean in there, he had serious doubts.

Patrick stepped closer and laid a hand on Tray's shoulder gently. "Dallas isn't going to harm her or take her," Patrick assured him. "I know you've claimed her for your own, Tray. I can see it in your eyes and so can Dallas, but you don't know what she's been through. She may not feel the same about you, and as alpha I will protect her, even from you if I have to." Patrick's words were sharp and there was a clear threat there, he was alpha, and he was strong.

Tray wanted to lash out at Patrick for even suggesting such a thing, but all he could do was nod. Tray would have to abide by Patrick's word as law unless he wanted to challenge him, which he didn't. He had no desire to run a pack, but he also knew that if Patrick tried to stand between him and this beautiful woman, he would rip Patrick's throat out and run off with her. Now was not the time for any of those things though, so he stayed silent and gritted his teeth as he looked down at the body of the female that belonged to him.

He felt it one hundred percent in his soul, and there was nothing Patrick or anyone else was going to do to keep them apart. When she woke up, she would agree, and she would tell everyone that she was his.

She had to.

Dallas came back with a blanket that smelled like it hadn't been washed in the last year, but Tray grabbed it with a grateful grunt anyway. He moved her more carefully than he'd handle a bomb as he wrapped her securely and lifted her in his arms. The feel of holding her, knowing he could run and be alone with her, knowing she was completely dependent upon him, knowing that all he had to do was lean forward slightly and he could press his lips to her skin. It was amazing and filled him with so much purpose and completeness it was terrifying. His life was hers now.

Dallas and Patrick shifted back to wolf, and they all headed through the woods to the waiting vehicle. They were able to ditch the old blanket and trade for one Patrick had stuffed in the back along with extra clothes for them all. Tray didn't bother dressing her in the clothes that would have been far too large, he just wrapped her tight in the blanket. As the sun was coming up, he had her settled in the back seat with her head in his lap. He stroked her hair gently as Patrick drove them away from the horror that had been her life for god knew how long. Away from the vampires of Atlantis and the Aristotle Society.

They were headed toward the safety of the pack and no doubt, a million questions. They'd been on a mission to help the Descendants of Atlantis with a little vampire problem. A werewolf's instincts were to protect humans, so when Julie, the leader of the Descendants, had called and said her sister had been kidnapped and vampires were closing in on their territory, they had of course agreed to help. Then they had taken Katherine, a Descendant and love of the vampire king, Ian's life, captive in hopes of solving the very desperate problem of keeping their loved ones safe during the full moon. She worked for the museum so maybe she could find the Blood Moonstone, and since the Descendants' Stone had found it's way into her museum, it wasn't crazy to assume. She'd agreed to help, though to be honest they hadn't really given her much choice in the matter. She'd been in a cell and they had threatened the life of her love.

They were returning with a female werewolf, a legend no one believed had ever really existed.

"Did Katherine find the Stone at the museum?" Tray asked as they drove. It seemed like so much less of an important issue when he had this woman in his lap, but he knew that for the rest of the pack it was of the utmost importance.

"No, but she said she would do some research on it. She was

pretty confident she'd be able to find it if it was sitting in some museum somewhere. They have databases that share information on their items, she just needs a little time to look into it."

"If her vamp boyfriend wasn't eaten by a monster because we left him in that prison," Dallas pointed out. "She won't be very helpful if he dies there."

"We were doing our job," Patrick said firmly.

"That makes two Descendants that get it on with vamps, do you think they're going back to them? Like history repeating itself and shit?" Dallas asked.

"I think that the vamps alive now are not the same as the ones that roamed after the sinking," Patrick said with a frown. "Well, literally they might be, but I think with Ian in charge the views have changed."

"So they aren't dangerous?" Dallas asked.

"Dangerous, yes. But monsters trying to rule the world? Probably not." Patrick said.

"Julie hates them," Dallas pointed out.

"Julie is following the old rules to the letter and when people refuse to grow and change, they die," Patrick said.

"Old rules set by the witches," Dallas mumbled. "Those bitches are nuts."

Patrick grunted agreement.

Tray stared out at the passing scenery and wondered what had become of the Descendants after they left. Did that monster, Norgis show up with his vampire friend, Jovi? Tray had smelled the faint scent of Norgis in the city, but knew it wasn't fresh. Probably Jovi, Ian's brother, had led the thing to The Descendants along with the Stone to enslave them. Rumor was Jovi was bitter about not being made king when their father died, and he wanted things back to the way they'd been with all the pretty little blood slaves. Every Descendant's worst fear. Too bad their leader, Julie, was such a bitch, otherwise maybe they would have stuck around to help out.

Maybe Katherine's vampires had gotten out of the cell and killed everyone in sight? It would be a more merciful ending than being Jovi's slaves.

Tray didn't trust bloodsuckers. He preferred them under the ocean not walking around near his territory, even if Ian claimed to be reformed and the clan that was in charge of Miami didn't cause much trouble. They still had to eat and that made a victim out of some unwilling human.

But Patrick was right, they weren't the dangerous monsters they once were. That didn't mean they should be allowed to roam free among the humans though. Jovi was proof of that, he wanted to destroy, to control and take and he'd released a monster to meet that goal.

If Tray didn't have this female to think about, he'd likely be volunteering to hunt Jovi and his monster down whether Patrick agreed or not. He looked down at her serene face bathed in sunlight and traced her nose and lips with a fingertip. He hadn't had something to live for in a long time.

They drove all day and she never woke up. He listened carefully to her breathing and heartbeat. He knew she was alive and likely healing some deep wounds both physical and mental now that she was free of that silver collar. It was a good sign that she was sleeping he had to remind himself often. A good thing that she felt comfortable and safe enough to let her body heal in such a vulnerable way with him.

After some discussion, they decided to head to a safehouse rather than anyone's town homes. There was no telling what she would need or how she would react when she did wake up and the farther from humans the better.

He wanted her to wake up with just him, wanted to keep her safe from the other werewolves too. Patrick wouldn't agree to leaving them alone though. Patrick and Dallas would stay with them just in case she woke up unhappy with the situation Tray was trying to push for. Tray agreed because he was certain she would agree that she was his. How could she not when he felt it so strongly? And once she agreed, no other would dare touch her, they wouldn't dare cross him.

"Maybe I should call Mary in," Patrick said when they got close. "She might appreciate another female around the house when she wakes up."

"Do you really want to expose your human wife to a possibly violent werewolf?" Tray pointed out, not because he really thought she would wake up and become violent, but because he didn't want more people around. He wanted as much alone time with her as he could get.

"It's too bad we don't have the Stone. Keeping her from shifting right off might be a good idea," Patrick said.

Tray didn't like that idea at all. She'd just been forced into one form for god knew how long. He never wanted her to feel that kind of powerlessness ever again. "If you're afraid of a starved female, I'm not sure you have what it takes to be alpha," Tray said.

Dallas growled in the front seat, not liking his alpha being challenged.

Patrick stayed calm and put a reassuring hand on Dallas' shoulder. That was why he was alpha; he had more ability to control his anger and werewolf than anyone Tray had ever seen.

"It doesn't matter because we don't have it, do we? With the three of us there, there's no way she will run out and attack anyone. Worst she'll do is damage the furniture. I won't call Mary in just yet, but if she wakes up and needs more than our male energy, you know she's the best choice unless you're anxious to announce her presence to the entire pack," Patrick said.

Tray nodded and Dallas settled. Mary was Patrick's wife and so he'd tell her all about this as soon as they spoke anyway, they had no secrets. Dallas didn't have a mate, so he didn't have anyone to tell. Any other female out there that knew about them was either the mate or daughter of another werewolf and if they started getting wind of a female werewolf, the news would spread through the pack faster than a wildfire. They all agreed that wasn't a good thing just yet.

They pulled up in front of the large cabin that the pack used on full moons. The place was a five-bedroom, three-bathroom, hunting cabin originally. They'd updated it and added a reinforced basement where they could restrain a wolf if needed, or in an emergency it could house a human in a saferoom no werewolf could break into. This is where they brought new wolves into the pack and where they held important meetings. Sometimes where they just gathered for a barbecue. He'd only been with Patrick's pack a few years, but it was as familiar to Tray as his own home, and he felt a sense of completeness as he carried the female over the threshold.

He took her upstairs to a room all the way at the end of the hall. It was his favorite because it had a small balcony and a view of a nearby river. She would wake up in a room filled with fresh air. He wanted her to know as soon as she woke up that she was somewhere safe and free. No chains or collars, no cage or bars. He didn't know what she'd been held in with those men, but he doubted it had been humane.

He laid her gently on the bed and stroked the hair away from her face. He pulled an extra blanket over her and opened the balcony doors. Then he sat in a chair and settled in to watch her. He would not leave her side until she woke. He nearly vibrated with the desire to hear her voice, to see her human eyes look at him.

"What is your name?" he wondered aloud.

* * *

Lilly jerked awake, sat up with a gasp and when she heard her human voice instead of her wolfy one, she gasped again. Her head spun as she tried to take in everything around her and then her hands were on her body. Oh her body! She had her body! She wasn't in wolf form. Her hands went to her neck and then she squealed in delight at the feel of nothing there.

"Good morning."

The voice had her scrambling off the bed and backing up to the wall. There sat the man she'd seen in the museum and again before blacking out. The wolf who had given himself up to be with her, who had looked at her with lust and possession, who had tried to save her... *had* saved her.

Tray.

She opened her mouth, but she wasn't sure she remembered how to talk. She closed her lips and ran her tongue around her human mouth, feeling her small blunt teeth. He just watched her and leaned forward looking eager. His eyes bore into her expectantly.

"What's your name?" he asked quietly.

"L—Lilly," she stuttered in a whisper. Her throat felt weird, and the sound of her own voice was foreign to her ears.

"Lilly," he breathed the word and his lips quirked up in a smile. "My name is Tray."

"I know," she said, suddenly unsure. She grabbed the blanket off the bed and pulled it up to cover her body. Werewolves weren't generally shy about nudity, but it had been a long time since she'd been in this form, and she found herself missing the cover of fur. She debated for a moment shifting but decided she wasn't sure she ever wanted to be a wolf again.

"When Glen died, what happened?" She looked around quickly, he was between her and a door that likely led into a hall-way, she'd never make it out that way, but she noted the open door behind her leading to a balcony and an obvious escape route. She relaxed slightly, knowing she could at least try to get away if he made a grab at her.

"We were able to sever the connection quick enough to save you. You're safe here, this is our pack's safehouse. No humans are close by."

"Your pack?" she asked, a little nervous.

"Right now it's just me, Patrick, the alpha, and Dallas here. But I can ask them to leave if you want," he assured her quickly. "You don't have to face anyone else if you're not ready."

"Can I leave?" she asked quietly, her gaze once again darting to the door he was near.

Tray stood and she took a step back, closer to the door behind her.

"Of course, Lilly. You are no prisoner. We wanted to get you away somewhere safe to heal and adjust."

"Okay," she said. It sounded reasonable and it sounded like exactly what she wanted to hear, but the look in his eyes said, you run, and I'll chase you to the ends of the earth, it was intense.

"Lilly, I am here to protect you and make sure you have whatever you need."

Lilly wasn't sure she liked the desperate tone to his voice. She clutched the blanket tighter to her body.

He shook his head, seeing her distress and he took a step back, away from her but closer to the bedroom door. "I mean you no harm, I swear it, but, Lilly, I see in you my life's mate, my only one. The moment I saw you in the museum, I knew you were the reason I breathe. When I held you in my arms as a human, I knew that you were the only reason I live. You are my everything."

Her eyes were wide, her heart beat faster, and panic swelled. He was looking at her like she was the sun and stars, and it scared the shit out of her. She couldn't handle it, she shifted to wolf and cowered from him, tail tucked between her legs, she scuttled under the bed even as she berated herself for being a coward.

"Fuck," she heard him hiss. "Don't move." Then his soft footsteps and the sound of a door told her he left the room.

She peeked out and saw that he'd left the bedroom door open. It led to a hallway like she'd assumed. She could leave now; she could run away while he was distracted. She could jump off the balcony, she doubted they were more than a floor up, but she knew she could survive at least three.

But where would she go?

Trying to think reasonably, she admitted that she didn't believe he meant her harm. It was just a lot that he was putting on her in this first meeting with words and she needed a minute to think. So she stayed there under the bed and waited to see what he would do next. She could always bite him and run away later.

No part of her believed he wouldn't follow successfully though.

Eight

TRAY RETURNED a moment later and sat on the floor near the bed.

She could smell fresh raw meat and her mouth watered. She heard chewing and knew he was eating it, damn him. Was his plan to torture her until she came out begging for food?

"I'll share," he said softly and threw a piece of meat under the bed. She snatched it up, swallowing it without tasting it. "Come on out and you can have as much as you want. I swear I mean you no harm, no one here does. I'd rather die than hurt you, Lilly," he whispered. "And I would kill anyone who tried to harm you."

She moved out from under the bed, but she didn't shift back to human. She didn't know what to say to his claims and if she was a wolf, she didn't have to say anything.

He smiled at her and held out the plate. There was a big hunk of raw meat on it. She grabbed it with her mouth and backed away, eating it in a few quick chomps.

"Good stuff, fresh too. Patrick and Dallas took down a deer right after we got here," he commented.

Lilly looked at him and decided she needed to pull up her big girl pants and talk to the guy. She shifted back to human and quickly grabbed a blanket off the bed to wrap around her body.

He smiled brightly and it lit up his blue eyes in a delightful way.

"I want to clean up," she said quietly.

"Of course," Tray said with a smile. "There's a bathroom right down the hall."

Her legs were a bit unsteady as she followed him out of the room and down a dim hallway. It smelled like many wolves and her heart started to race, her breath came in pants, and she wanted to shift and bolt. He said it was just him and two others at the moment but what if he was lying, what if there were more lurking nearby, ready to pounce on the chance of a female werewolf too weak to properly defend herself?

Tray seemed to sense her distress because his back stiffened and he stopped walking, then turned slowly as if he feared he would frighten her away. Concern was etched all over his features as he looked at her and lifted his palms to show he wasn't a threat.

"What is it, Lilly?"

"I—I—how many wolves are here?" she stammered, tears stinging her eyes and her grip on the blanket iron tight.

"Just you, me, and two others. I swear that's all. This is a pack-house though, so you can smell the others, I know. No one else is here now and no one is going to harm you."

She nodded but her heart didn't settle. She felt vulnerable in this form, and it was such an unexpected feeling she knew she wasn't handling it well. She'd never felt vulnerable in her father's pack in either form after her initial turning and as a wolf she had weapons at the ready. Like this, here, she was at Tray's mercy, and she didn't know if she could trust him.

He motioned to the door. "Bathroom," he said softly.

A jingling sound filled the small space, and he pulled a small silver thing from his pocket and frowned at it then pushed something and shoved it back in his pocket.

"What year is it?" she whispered, afraid to know.

"Two thousand twenty-three," he said with a sympathetic look.

She gasped, a hundred years had passed since she was taken, a hundred fucking years of her life stolen. Was her father even still alive? The likelihood seemed less plausible than ever. Would any of his pack remember that she'd ever existed? So much time had passed and more than she ever would have imagined without her realizing it. How much of the time had she actually not been aware of what was happening? She'd thought maybe she'd lost a day or two here and there to the blackness of nothing, but maybe it was more like months and years.

Tray's face was full of concern as she wrestled with the reality of time but the fact that he didn't press her to explain what was going through her mind right then made her appreciate him. She tried to give him a smile but knew it was probably lopsided and shaky.

He pursed his lips as if he were holding back what he wanted to say, then motioned into the bathroom. "Shower there, towels should be in the cabinet, and I'll find something for you to wear. We have extra clothes here but it's all men's and large. We'll make something work for now though and I can send one of the others to town for something more appropriate."

She nodded and eyes wide, stared at the bathroom. It was so bright and white, so clean. She couldn't wait to stand under the hot water. She stepped into the bathroom, and he breathed deeply as she passed him. When she pulled the door shut between them, she saw a flash of worry in his eyes and for a brief moment she thought he was going to insist the door stayed open, or that he had to be in there with her.

But he didn't say anything, and she locked the door when it closed, not that it would keep a werewolf out. It did make her relax just a bit more.

She opened drawers and cabinets, finding towels, robes, and

toiletries of all kinds. It was well stocked, and she ran her hands over everything, taking it all in and wrapping her mind around the fact that she was here, she wasn't in that basement cage, and she was in human form. Everything looked so different from what she remembered. Nothing was quite the same, but she knew what it was. She could read of course, but it drove home the fact that she'd missed a lot in the time with the Aristotle Society. Time had moved on around her and she was in a world now that she didn't completely know. How hard was it going to be for her to adjust? Would she be able to find a place for herself in this modern world?

She didn't have answers, so she tried to stop asking herself questions. She managed to avoid looking into the mirror during her perusal and as she stepped into the shower. She was afraid of what she'd see there. Would she even recognize her own face after a hundred years as a wolf?

She didn't recognize her body, that was for sure. Mostly because of the stripes of red scars that wrapped around her torso, probably her back too. She traced a line from her right hip to just under her left breast where it disappeared around to her back. The silver chains that were wrapped around her for so long, rubbing off her fur and skin had left these. She wasn't sure if they would ever heal. She may never be free of the evidence of captivity. But at least she was alive to see the evidence, at least she was human and musing over the crossover of wolf injury to human body.

At least she had a chance to see if they would fade to nothing. She drew strength from that knowledge.

It took her a minute to figure out the knobs in the shower, but when the spray finally came out hot and hard, she giggled with delight. She let it soak into her for fifteen minutes before picking up the typically unscented soap to wash her body and hair. Were-wolves didn't use anything scented if they could help it, it messed with their ability to blend with nature and to track prey. She gloried in the feel of suds in her unfamiliar long hair and when her hands slid over her body, her nipples perked, and her thighs quivered.

She hadn't had a sexual release in all the time she'd been a wolf, and parts of her at least were eager to feel that again. Her hands moved over her skin sensually, giving her nipples a gentle pluck. She couldn't stop the small moan from rushing out of her throat at the sensation. She moved her hands lower, cupping her mound and sliding a finger to the sweet spot. It was so sensitive, so ready for her attention and she was quivering and gasping in no time at all.

It was the fastest orgasm she'd ever given herself.

She shuddered under the hot spray for a moment longer as her body came back to her, then she turned off the water and stepped out into the steamy room. She'd just reclaimed another piece of herself and she let a couple tears of satisfaction slide out as she pulled a fluffy towel from the cabinet. It might be a small thing, but like walking on two legs, owning her body and its reactions, and giving herself a needed release told her she was alive and she was in control.

The towel was a treat as she rubbed it over her body and up to her long hair. When had her hair ever been this long? She'd always kept it short and perky, so much easier to take care of.

The mirror was fogged over so she dared a look. The shadowy shape she saw there was thinner than it should have been and paired with the long hair, she didn't recognize herself. She frowned and took a steadying breath, then wiped a hand across the mirror, revealing her clear reflection.

Staring into her familiar gold eyes, she frowned again. Her cheeks were sunken, her eyes had dark circles under them, and her skin was pale. But it was her, and it was human. She couldn't quite believe it still, but she managed a small smile for her reflection as she pulled a comb through her wet locks. She found a pair of scissors and started to cut off chunks of the heavy hair. She cut and trimmed until it was a cute bob just above her shoulders.

Now when she looked into the mirror she felt more like herself. She flushed the hair and wiped up the mess, then pulled on a robe she found hanging on a hook and stared at the bathroom door.

She could smell him out there waiting for her and her cheeks reddened at the realization that he had probably heard her pleasuring herself in the shower. It was a natural thing though, and she refused to be embarrassed. So she notched up her chin and opened the door.

* * *

As soon as the bathroom door had closed, Tray rushed to find something she could wear. He rummaged through drawers they all shared and pulled out a t-shirt and a pair of sweats that had a drawstring. It would have to work.

"How is she?" Patrick asked, startling him from behind.

Tray turned with clothes in hand and a scowl on his face. "Her name is Lilly; she'll need appropriate clothing and lots of good meat. She's—" he paused trying to decide what to say, *perfect, mine, not to be bothered,* all ran through his head, but he knew that wouldn't satisfy Patrick. "She's frightened. I don't know what has happened to her or how long she was there, but she's scared." And it killed him to know he couldn't do anything about her past, couldn't take painful memories away for her.

Patrick nodded and moved so Tray could leave the bedroom and walk back toward the closed bathroom door. The shower was running now, and he itched to be in there with her. His mind filled with images of her naked wet body, and he growled.

"You need to keep yourself under control," Patrick warned.

Tray bared his teeth at his alpha but didn't make a sound.

"I want to talk to her when she's out and ready. I'll send Dallas to town for supplies, clothes, and food, but we will hunt again soon too, the fresh meat will help her heal faster." Patrick paused and took a deep breath. "She'll bleed soon, I'll have Dallas pick up supplies for that as well."

Tray gritted his teeth and fisted his hands. He wanted to punch Patrick in the face for smelling her, for knowing something so intimate about his woman.

Patrick's eyes were on him, and they were fierce. "She is not yours unless she wants to be, Tray. You said it yourself; you have no idea what she's been through, and she is afraid. A possessive dominating male is not what she needs right now. She's my pack unless she doesn't want to be and I protect my pack, even from itself."

"She needs to know she's safe, and I will be making sure she stays that way," Tray said. He wouldn't lie to his alpha, and to say he'd leave her alone would be a lie, but making her know she was safe, that was his biggest concern right now. If she tried to run off, if she disappeared, he would break. He had to make sure she felt safe with him.

Patrick nodded and headed downstairs, but Tray knew he wouldn't go far. Patrick really was looking out for her best interest and that fact was the only thing keeping Tray calm in the face of his demands and warnings.

Tray leaned against the bathroom door and listened to the sounds of her washing. When he heard her gasp and moan, he nearly ripped through the door. He gripped the trim and heard it crack as he restrained himself. Thank the gods the others were outside right now and couldn't possibly have heard her. His body reacted, hardening and yearning. He should be the one drawing those sounds from her lips, he should be swallowing her desire as she trembled against him.

By the time she opened the door wearing a fluffy white robe and her hair freshly cropped, he was in control of himself again, but the rush of hot air scented with her sweet release hit him like a slap and he rushed past her into the bathroom and opened the window. He didn't want the scent of her pleasure to drift through the house for the others to catch. At least not until it was mixed with his own, then it would stake his claim and he would be proud to shove it in their noses.

When he turned back to her, she was gripping her robe tightly and her bright gold eyes were wide with shock.

"You filled the room with your scent, you'll have to be more careful. I am not the only male in this house," he snapped and handed her the clothes he'd found. "Put these on and I will feed you again," he ordered and walked back out of the bathroom, shutting the door between them. He knew he'd spoken too harshly, that she didn't deserve that kind of treatment, but he couldn't help himself. Until she was fully claimed by him, he'd be animalistic in his need to keep the others away.

He managed some deep breathing and calmed himself. When she opened the door cautiously a second time, he knew his face was a smooth mask, but underneath he was burning with the desire to claim her.

The black t-shirt he'd found was huge on her, but she'd tied it up on the side managing to make it look less ridiculous. The sweats were so big and so long that she'd had to roll and tie them at the waist, and they still slipped down over her feet like socks.

Tray smiled and shook his head. This tiny thing was the most beautiful specimen he'd ever seen in his entire life. He reached out and tucked a lock of her shortened hair behind her ear. "Why did you cut it?"

She shrugged. "I always kept it short so it would stay out of the way. Long hair just doesn't suit me."

"It grew while you were a wolf?" he asked, surprised.

"I guess so," she shrugged.

He had so many questions, but they could wait. He needed to feed her again. "Follow me, I'll make you dinner."

She padded along behind him through the hallway and down the stairs. Her arms were crossed over her body in a nervous gesture that made his heart ache. The only thing he could do to truly convince her that she was safe was to show her with his actions. So he led her to the kitchen and motioned to a stool at the counter. He could hear Patrick outside chopping wood and a quick glance told him the car was gone, so Dallas must have headed into town.

The kitchen was large with lots of windows. Sunlight filled the space, and he watched her move to one and close her eyes as it hit her face.

"The sun feels amazing," she whispered.

"How long since you've felt the sun?"

She shook her head. "I don't know. Time was lost to me. I never would have guessed a hundred years had passed since I was captured."

Tray nearly choked at that, a hundred years. She'd been held captive for a hundred years. How had no one known, how had she survived? Anger boiled through him, and he had to distract himself before she saw his face twisted in hatred for the ones who had done that to her. He poured her a glass of milk and pulled a hunk of the deer they'd brought down earlier out of the fridge. He set them on the counter, and she sat in front of them with an eager smile.

"Eat," he said.

She grabbed the glass and drank it all greedily.

Tray laughed and filled it again as her cheeks reddened in embarrassment. "There's as much as you want," he assured her.

"Are you eating?" she asked as she looked at the large portion of meat he'd put on her plate.

"Later, I'm going to make a salad first, you need the fresh meat mostly, but some veggies won't hurt either," he explained. "At least that's what my mother always insisted," he said with a laugh. He felt so much joy in providing for her. He pulled out vegetables to start making a salad and heard her chewing the meat and gulping more of the milk. His heart filled with pleasure.

No doubt providing for one's mate was the ultimate in happiness.

He filled her glass again and gave her a large bowl of salad and another hunk of meat, then made his own plate and settled in beside her. They ate in silence, and he was impressed by the amount of food she was able to put away, no doubt it spoke to how little she'd been given during captivity. Just barely enough to survive, he assumed, and hatred filled him.

He would seek out Brandon and he would rip out the bastard's throat, burn down his business, and make sure that no one ever captured another werewolf.

He froze and his fork dropped to the ground as a horrific realization filled him.

Lilly went on alert immediately, she shifted to werewolf and growled viciously, eyes darting around, she stood at his feet protectively, searching for the danger that had made him gasp.

Patrick ran inside, ax in hand, "What is it?" he demanded, looking from Lilly to Tray.

Tray gulped and looked at Patrick. "We didn't take the collar and ring, for fuck's sake, Patrick, we didn't take them. He can do it again! He isn't dead, he has enough knowledge and the tools."

"Shit," Patrick hissed and relaxed, lowering the ax as he realized the danger wasn't immediate.

Lilly whined and sat, looking up at him with her big gold wolfy eyes.

"She's protective of you," Patrick pointed out with a huff of disbelief, then turned and left the house. "We'll get Brandon and his fucking supplies," Patrick called back as the door shut.

Tray looked down at Lilly and smiled. "We can protect each other I think, and we will stop Brandon from harming any other werewolf. Now back to human, we need to talk."

Lilly glanced down at her ripped clothing and back up at Tray making no move to shift back to human.

"You're shy?"

She whined.

He kind of liked that she was shy. He didn't want her to hide her body from him, but he didn't necessarily want her comfortable being naked in front of others. "Follow me," he said with a laugh and headed upstairs. He rummaged for a change of clothes then took them to the bedroom where she'd woken up and set them on the bed. "I'll wait for you downstairs," he said softly, petted her head gently, and left the room, closing the door behind him.

He couldn't wait for the day that a closed door would be unnecessary. For the day she welcomed his gaze on her naked body.

For now he would be satisfied with the knowledge that she trusted him to feed and clothe her, wanted to protect him, and was here in this house with him willingly.

Nine

LILLY SHIFTED and put the clothes on quickly. She was on edge, tuned to the feelings of Tray. His little shocked thought had nearly had her attacking shadows. She needed to control herself better, needed to remember that she was safe now. Tray made her feel safe even as his intensity frightened her. Patrick seemed calm, most alphas were, and he hadn't started demanding anything from her. But would he? Would he want her for his own? He was the alpha here, wouldn't he want the best prize? Which she wouldn't be once he knew she couldn't carry a child, if he didn't already know. Maybe he did, maybe that was why he hadn't already taken her from Tray.

She tried to stop her thoughts from circling around the horrible possibilities. She was safe, no one had tried to harm her. She was being clothed and fed and she could shift at will and there was nothing stopping her from going outside and running away. Nothing except a couple male werewolves who were stronger and faster than her. She knew they wouldn't let her run if they didn't want her to. She wasn't strong enough to evade them. She would just wait, get more of her strength back and see what their intentions really were. If she needed to escape, she'd do everything in her power to escape. She wasn't going to be a willing prisoner now that she was free.

She hurried across the hall to use the bathroom before sneaking back downstairs.

She heard their voices and paused halfway down.

"We have to go back," Patrick was saying.

"I agree, but I'm not taking her anywhere near that shit. You said it yourself; she has to be traumatized, what do you think would happen if she saw that freak again?" Tray said.

"I'd rip out his throat and eat his heart," Lilly said, descending the rest of the way down the stairs.

The two men froze and looked at her. Patrick's face was pleasantly surprised, and Tray's was angry.

"I won't let you expose yourself to such a risk," Tray said.

"You aren't my alpha," she said and turned to Patrick. "Neither are you actually. I appreciate that you two helped me, but I'm not part of your pack and I don't have to listen to either one of you."

Tray's face reddened as his anger bubbled.

Patrick nodded and held up his hands. "True, you don't have to do anything you don't want, which includes becoming part of my pack, though you would be welcomed. Either way, while you are here under my care, I will protect you as if you are part of my pack. I won't make any demands of you, Lilly. That's not the kind of alpha I am. Why don't you come sit, and tell us everything, then we can decide what's best to do next. If your pack is still out there, would you like us to locate them?"

Tray let out a short low growl, but Patrick seemed to be ignoring him.

"Yes, my father was alpha, but it's been so long. I don't even know if he's still alive." Her voice caught with emotion.

"Come sit," Patrick prompted again and gave Tray a little shove in the direction of the couch.

Lilly sat in a chair rather than taking the seat on the couch next to Tray and he moved as soon as she sat so that he was as close to her as he could be. Patrick rolled his eyes and took up a seat on the other side of the coffee table giving her plenty of space.

"I was held by the Aristotle Society for a hundred years."

Patrick's eyes went wide at her admission.

"Let's start from the beginning, shall we? Lilly, tell us how is it that you are a werewolf. There hasn't been a confirmed female werewolf ever, it's all legend and myth."

Lilly shook her head and looked down at her clutched hands, then took a deep breath. She told them of growing up with her parents, her mother's unsuccessful turning, and her own amazing success.

"Your father was alpha, maybe those genetics helped guide you through it," Patrick pointed out.

"Could be, there were a few who tried after me, none with any success and so they stopped allowing any to try. A few still did, in secret, but still, there was no success and the werewolves who tried turning their wives and daughters were punished. It was more important to have breeding humans who knew about us than to have more female werewolves. Especially once it was obvious I couldn't breed." She went still after that admission. Waiting to see how they would react. Would they suddenly decide she wasn't worth the trouble? Would Tray stop looking at her like she was the single most important thing in the world.

Why did she hope he wouldn't?

"That part of the legend is true then?" Tray asked casually, as if it didn't matter in the least.

She felt more relief than she probably should have as she met his gaze. "Much to the disappointment of my father, and his pack," she said and her cheeks reddened. "Probably because of the full moon forced changes. Any possibility of pregnancy could never survive that shifting back and forth." She shrugged. "Or at least that's my theory. Everything else seems to work normally. But even in wolf form without being able to change to human I was never able to carry a pregnancy, which really pissed off the Aristotle guys who took me."

She saw Tray and Patrick exchange a meaningful look but neither of them spoke up so she continued her story. She told of her capture and the years of solitude after the others had died.

"As far as we can tell, Brandon is the last of The Society. He was working alone aside from the cousin who overdosed. No rumors of their existence have popped up for thirty years or more so it's doubtful there are any others," Patrick said.

"Is that why the vampires are back?" Lilly asked.

"They aren't back, not really. Most still reside underwater as they should," Tray assured her.

"I tracked one in the city a few nights before I came across you guys," she said.

"Miami is vampire territory, a zone of protection between Atlantis and the rest of the world. A small coven lives there permanently, and Ian came up recently because his brother let a monster out," Patrick said.

Lilly nodded. "I think I smelled that too."

"Not our problem," Tray said. "We have a deal with the Descendants of Atlantis, we will stand with them against the vampires if attacked and if the vampires are roaming too far from Miami. We helped them capture the vamps near their place and we got the girl who might be able to find the Blood Moonstone for us as a bonus."

"Is that what you were doing at the museum?"

"Yes, we hope to be able to hold off the change again. We want to be able to be with our loved ones without fear," Patrick said.

Lilly's eyes widened. "Did she? Does she know where it is?"

"No, but she's promised to keep trying, she has connections," Patrick said with fierce hope. "With it, you might even be able to carry a child, stay human through the pregnancy."

Lilly felt her throat close up, with hope or fear she wasn't sure.

She met Tray's gaze and saw it all there. The hope and desire for her to have his children.

She jumped up and backed away, suddenly afraid, feeling the chains of control trying to wrap around her.

Tray stood quickly. "It's not what you think, Lilly. This has nothing to do with you. We didn't even know about you when we went after it. This is all about families, wives and human children who can stay safe on full moons."

"But you think it can and you want that. I can see it in your eyes," she whispered, looking from Tray back to Patrick, he was the alpha, he would be the one to make the call, to force her to breed for them.

"I know how it seems," Patrick said softly. "I assure you I have no interest in forcing you into any situation, Lilly. *If* you wanted to join my pack and *if* you wanted to try to have a child, we would be cautiously optimistic with the Stone, but I'm not stupid. We don't know if you could or what it would be even if you did. There is no record of werewolves breeding ever, not even a legend like the female werewolves includes children."

"The Descendants probably know," Tray pointed out and they swung their heads around to look at him. "They have records dating back to the sinking. If there was ever an occurrence of breeding successfully before the Blood Moonstone was stolen from us, they would know of it. We could be sure," Tray said.

Patrick kept his gaze carefully on Lilly. "Doesn't matter, Lilly is her own person, her own wolf."

"Of course she is but—" Tray started to say.

"Nothing," Patrick snapped. "Tray, you have claimed her in your mind only and I am close to sending you away. Watch yourself, I won't put her through any more than she's already been through. Were you even listening to her story? Are you comprehending the implications of what she's been through?"

Lilly didn't sit, just looked from one to the other, unsure. She wanted to trust Patrick, but she didn't know if she could, not really

He was basically a stranger. And Tray, he was something else entirely, so raw and so sure of things she wasn't at all sure about. On a purely physical level she was attracted to him, but his intensity scared her, the future she saw in his eyes terrified her.

The sound of a car approaching had them all jolting. Tray was instantly by her side.

"Dallas is back," Patrick said. "We can discuss what to do about the collar and ring."

"I want to go back for it," Lilly said. "I want to know that the things are destroyed."

"I will be honored to have you with us when we go," Patrick said.

Dallas came into the house with his arms full of bags. "Clothes for the female," he declared happily.

"You didn't have to do that," Lilly said quietly as she took the bag he handed her.

"Apparently I did," he said and shot a glare at Patrick. "What the alpha says, goes, you know."

"Thank you," she said as she peered into the bag and saw pretty pinks and purples, yellow and black. "I'm sure these will fit better than what I've got on," she laughed. The sweats were at least five times too big and so was the shirt. She felt like she was trying to wear blankets as clothes, and it was ridiculous. A part of her was excited to look pretty and she hurried upstairs with the bag.

"Wait, this one's got tampons. Patrick said you need them soon," Dallas shouted up and held another smaller bag out.

"What?"

"Tampons. Patrick says you'll bleed soon."

Her cheeks went bright red, and she clutched the bag of clothes to her chest. "I—I don't know about that but, what the hell is a tampon and what does it have to do with anything?"

The men exchanged uncomfortable looks.

"Um, well, I guess it's a little more modern than your time. But there's probably a diagram inside the package," Tray said uncomfortably. "Just take it, you don't have to use them, but look at it, then you'll know."

Tray took the bag from Dallas and handed it to Lilly, who grabbed it and fled up the stairs and to the bedroom feeling embarrassed and inept.

She sat on the bed and pulled out the blue box from the bag and opened it up suspiciously. She pulled out a long thin package. It was slick like plastic, how the hell was this supposed to help with her monthly bleed?

She bit her lip anxiously. The world had changed around her and there were probably a million new things she had no idea how to interact with. She set the box aside to deal with later and started pulling items out of the clothing bag.

She decided on a long black skirt and a purple sleeveless top, then hurried to put them on. Only realizing afterwards that underwear hadn't been included in the bag. She supposed that was fine, she would get her own. Somewhere, somehow... she fell back on the bed with despair. She had no money, no identification, nothing that really belonged to her. She was helpless aside from the generosity of Patrick and his pack. Unless she wanted to risk taking off on her own. Which seemed like a bad idea, as a human or werewolf she was likely to get into trouble. Not every alpha would be as understanding as Patrick seemed to be. As willing to let her make decisions for herself.

Lilly rubbed her arms and a tear rolled down her cheek as she accepted a moment of self-pity. She was at the mercy of this pack. She needed to make sure they didn't abandon her. In some ways she'd been safer in Brandon's cage and that was a horrible thought she quickly pushed away. This was all scary and different, but it had to be better than that cage.

She pulled herself together, wiped her face and walked back downstairs. She found the men settled around the living room, silent. They all stood when she walked in. Dallas gave her a bright

COURTNEY DAVIS

smile and whistle of approval. Patrick nodded with a smile and
Tray's eyes raked up and down her body possessively.

"Thank you for the clothes, it feels weird to wear clothes again,
but ones that fit are much better than the borrowed stuff."

"You look great," Patrick said. "Now everyone sit. We need to
figure out what to do next."

Ten

BRANDON SPENT the entire day in the hospital. Apparently, a couple missing digits wasn't an emergency. They gave him some ice and made him sit in the waiting room. His head spun and he'd have given his left nut for some strong pain killers. He knew Rylee had something good back at the trailer and if Glen hadn't found it, he'd guilt her into sharing some.

"Wasted my entire day off," Rylee complained.

"Well maybe you could have used the time to learn about nursing instead of sucking off doctors for pills and cash," Brandon hissed as he stared down at his bandaged hand.

Rylee smiled and looked at herself in the rearview mirror. "I made more today than I would have if I'd worked at the club. Might make a regular appearance there, doctors are rich and desperate because of the long hours."

Brandon just grunted and shifted in his seat. Glen told him how often Rylee had to get penicillin at the clinic, and he wondered how many doctors were going home with a brand-new itch tonight. He'd never risk his pride and joy in something like that, no matter how desperate he was.

"The shit they gave me isn't working," he complained as he popped another pill and dry swallowed it.

"Pills are for beginners," Rylee agreed. "But they sell well, these babies will have my rent paid for three months." She patted her purse.

Brandon pushed the seat back and closed his eyes, letting his mind drift as they drove. The sun was down, and he had his own goldmine waiting for him. Those two wolves were going to make him rich with pups.

He must have fallen asleep because the next thing he knew, they were lurching to a stop and Rylee was screaming as she ran across the dirt driveway to the body of Glen laying facedown. "Call 911!" she shouted and rolled him over.

Brandon got out of the car with a wobble, his head fuzzed from sleep and painkillers. He walked over to his cousin and shook his head. He'd seen a few dead bodies in his life, some overdoses and one stabbing. He knew it was too late for Glen, way too late.

"Fuck," Brandon said and stumbled to the van, hurrying around to the back, he threw the doors open. "No!" he screamed at the empty space. "You fucking worthless bastard," he hissed as he slammed the doors shut. He walked back toward Glen and Rylee. She was frantically calling for help on the phone and glaring at him.

He kneeled down in the dirt and picked up the two silver collars and looked around until he found the ring a foot from Glen's body.

"I never should have left an idiot in charge."

"What?" Rylee asked, frantic as she began chest compressions on Glen.

Brandon didn't answer, just walked over to the van and got in. He drove off to the sound of approaching sirens. He didn't need to be involved with another overdose death.

He drove back to the shop a little surprised he made it safely as his head spun from lack of sleep, loss of blood, and the pain pills. Luckily, he was used to surviving under similar conditions.

"Whoa, dude are you okay?" Lance, one of his part time employees asked as he stumbled through the shop to his office.

Brandon just waved a hand at the kid. "Fine, I'll be in my office taking a nap."

"Sure thing, I can stick around for a couple more hours but then I am out. I came in and opened the place before noon so..." Lance trailed off as Brandon slammed his office door.

The kid was reliable, came in when asked and all, but Brandon didn't like him much. He was too young, too much of a pushover with customers. But when you were supposed to be open twenty-four hours, it took more than two people to run the place, and now Glen was gone.

"Fuck!" Brandon cursed and fell into his chair. He was going to miss his cousin and even though it was obviously an overdose death, he blamed those stupid wolves, no doubt they could have chosen to save him and hadn't. He would get them back, and then he would make them suffer.

He pulled himself back together and took out the book his father had left him. He stared down at the heavy leatherbound thing that he'd never been much interested in before. He'd known all he needed to know from watching how his father dealt with the wolf, which wasn't much, and reading wasn't really his thing anyway. He'd quit school at eighth grade when they wanted to put him in special classes to catch up. He refused to be marked as stupid for the rest of his life just because the idiot teachers couldn't tell him how to learn right. He'd done fine for himself without their useless diploma.

Aristotle's Wolves, the title proclaimed in shining gold lettering. It creaked as it opened and the smell of old paper hit him, making his nose crinkle. His desire for drugs to dull the pain of his hand was replaced by a burning need for revenge. He would find that bitch and her boyfriend and he would destroy them, slowly, locked in his cage and forced to do his bidding. It was his new mission, killing vamps would come second to their suffering. And anyone else who'd helped them, did those other two werewolves come after them? Were there other werewolves? He'd been led to believe the werewolves had pretty much died out, but apparently, they were just hiding. The Aristotle Society hadn't captured a new wolf since before his father's generation. Then in the thirties a bunch of them had died out, their captives halved in like two months from some kind of sickness. Brandon tried to think of what his father had told him other than that. A few of the wolves had starved to death, refusing to eat, a couple killed each other in a fight over something or other. Eventually it was just her. That bitch might have been the last one captured, but he wasn't sure. For a long time it was just her and no rumors of others anywhere in his lifetime.

Now he knew that there were at least the four, though one may have died after being shot. Just in case, he would need two more collars and a way to track them down. That's what he was hoping to find in the book. How had his ancestors caught the damn things to begin with? He opened to the first page.

We, the members of the Aristotle Society, men of wealth, power, and mind, have traded our scholarly ways for days of training. We have been called to duty by the goddess Elantra to save the earth from the vampires who refuse to stay beneath the sea. The earth beasts, the wolf men, are helping us so that we might defend our shores. We will work together; we will keep the chosen safe.

Brandon shook his head, *wolf men?* "Werewolves," he whispered to himself as he tried to understand the opening paragraph. With a grunt he sat back in the chair and rubbed his eyes, this was going to take a while. He flipped back to the front but there was no chapter list and no indication of where to find information in the back. A quick look told him that it must have been written in real time as they learned and developed more like a journal than an instruction manual.

Skipping most of the book, he opened to a random page toward the back and started reading. He skimmed a few pages. These were entries from the twenties, and he found his grandfather's name, Thomas Plant. He stopped there and read.

The wolf men are unpredictable, full of pride and refuse to listen to reason. It has become increasingly apparent in these modern times that we must find a way to bind them to us. They will let our men die in favor of protecting their own. They hate the bloodsucking monsters as much as us, but they will sacrifice us for their own end. They do not wish to stay on guard against invasion, they see no need to be battle ready with us.

Our easy camaraderie is coming to an end, and we will seek the guidance of the Goddess Elantra's people for assistance. There must be a way to bind the beasts to us so that we can keep the world safe. I will go and seek the coven by the sea and beg their magic. The chosen have given me guidance to find them, the same ones who spelled their home to be invisible. I have been warned to approach with caution, that they are not trusting of outsiders, but I am not an outsider, I am one of their soldiers and I will bring with me tales of terror that will surely become reality if they don't give us the tools to control the beasts.

The book was blank after that, and Brandon frowned. Obviously, his grandfather had been successful but it gave him no clues to follow from here. He shut the book and shoved it away from him. Then he sat up and smiled darkly. He picked up the phone and dialed a number, his hand shaking.

The voice that picked up was unexpected, a deep male voice with an accent he couldn't place.

"Hello," it drawled.

Brandon hesitated only a moment. "This is Brandon, and I am looking for Julie."

There was a dark chuckle. "She's a little tied up right now, what can I do for you?"

"I need to know how to track a werewolf down and I need more collars. Do you have access to the Goddess Elantra and her people?"

"Elantra," the voice snarled. "No Goddess, she. But it's interesting to hear she's been touting herself as one all this time."

"Whatever she is, she helped the Aristotle Society once and I need it again."

"The Aristotle Society is quite into killing vampires, isn't it?"

Brandon stiffened. "It is what I do," he agreed, too dumb to cover his tracks now.

"Not very well," the voice laughed darkly. "Run and hide, I'll come for you next."

The line went dead, and Brandon shook with fear. That was one of them, they are taking over the world!

He had to prepare.

* * *

Lilly listened while the men discussed the best course of action. It would take hours to drive back to Miami and then they'd have to search the trailer as well as the shop and Brandon's house, if they could find it. Brandon was likely to be around one of those places and they all agreed he needed to be taken out for his stupidity alone.

"But we don't need to rush off tonight, it's been a long day. I say we sleep, alert the pack to these developments, and get an update from the Descendants as well. I want to know where the bloodsuckers and Norgis are before we head into possible danger."

"I won't risk taking Lilly back to the city if Norgis is roaming about," Tray said.

"That's not a problem any of us need to be a part of," Patrick agreed. "We'll let them clean up their own mess as long as the humans aren't becoming victims."

Lilly wouldn't argue with steering clear of the monster she'd scented in the city, she had no desire to try and be a hero to the humans until she was back to full strength. She *was* very interested in what the Descendants might know though. "The Descendants, they are the ones who might have information that . . . uh, information that I might like to have?" Lilly said, her gaze darting briefly to Dallas. She didn't want to bring up having a baby in front of him if he didn't already know about that conversation or hadn't already figured it out for himself. She wasn't going to put the idea in his head.

Tray gave her an eager look. "Yes. We can go there too. I think its information we all would like to have."

Patrick nodded. "Julie owes me for returning her sister unharmed, and the Descendants shouldn't be hoarding knowledge about us."

"If we aren't leaving tonight, I can make dinner," Lilly offered, wanting to be helpful. Even though she'd just eaten, she was hungry. It was as if the idea of food being available had unlocked years of starvation she needed to make up for.

"I'll help," Tray said and when Dallas made a rude noise, Tray punched his shoulder.

As Lilly moved awkwardly around the kitchen trying to remember how to do simple things like make a pot of rice and steam some vegetables, Tray was right there, anticipating her needs and he didn't once get frustrated when she couldn't figure something out like how to light the stove. Which apparently didn't need to be lit, it was electric. That was a little embarrassing.

It felt so good to be doing human things, things she never thought she'd do again. "This is nice," she said, her voice full of emotion as she diced carrots for salad.

"Cutting vegetables?" Tray asked.

Lilly laughed. "All of this. Making food, walking on two legs." She kicked out a foot and smiled. "Wearing clothes. I think I gave up hope of ever doing anything outside of that cell and my wolf form."

Tears stung her eyes and her throat clamped as she felt the weight of that hopelessness again. Her hand shook and the knife slipped. "Oh!" she hissed and stuck a bleeding finger into her mouth as tears for her past self rolled down her face, but at least she could pretend it was about her finger.

"Lilly," Tray said softly and pulled her in for a hug. "You're safe now, I swear you are safe and free, and I won't let anyone take that away from you again, not ever."

She shuddered in his arms and tried to believe his words, but she just kept seeing the possessiveness in his eyes, the glimmer of hope when the Stone was mentioned.

"I cut my finger," she mumbled around the digit in her mouth.

"Oh, let me see." He turned her around and pulled her finger out of her mouth. Blood welled up from the cut and Tray frowned. He led her to the sink and washed the finger then pulled a first aid kit from under the sink. "You're not the first wolf to cut a finger in the kitchen," Tray said as he bandaged the finger. "But you are certainly the prettiest."

She looked down at the bandage and felt a warmth build in her belly. He was kind and gentle, very handsome and he smelled so good. It had been so long since anyone had done something for her, so long since she'd felt cared for. Not just a tool, not a weapon or an asset, a person with emotions and needs and desires.

Another tear slid down her cheek.

"Does it still hurt? Maybe you need a stitch," Tray said, wiping the tear from her cheek. "Or maybe a hug?" he said quietly, realizing that the tears weren't about the finger at all.

She knew it was probably a bad idea, she shouldn't lead him on, but she really did need a hug, so she leaned into him. When his arms went around her she felt protected. She breathed in his scent, and she knew she wasn't alone, and it felt good.

She looked up into his eyes and she saw her future. Mate, kids, the end.

She pushed him away and turned back to the carrots. "I guess I'll throw these ones out, I bled all over them," she mumbled and busied herself with dinner prep to avoid looking at him and answering the question there.

She didn't want the kind of commitment he was offering her right now. She wasn't sure she would ever want it. She didn't know where she fit in the world anymore, and the last thing she wanted to do was make decisions while she was still so unsettled, feeling so vulnerable and honestly, a little scared.

She had no one and nothing.

The meal turned out great. Raw meat, rice, steamed veggies and salad. They ate and she asked questions about the world. They told her the human history of the last hundred years and technological advancements. "Wow, how have we stayed hidden?" she wondered aloud when Dallas pulled out his cellular phone and typed something in it that then allowed him to pull up an image of earth from space and zoom in on various places around the globe.

"We've definitely had to work harder at it," Patrick said with a frown.

"Where did you grow up?" Dallas asked, ready to type in a command on the magical little device.

"North of here, Georgia. My father had a large plot of land where the pack mostly surrounded us."

"No pack in Georgia anymore but I can show you what it looks like anyway," Dallas said and started poking at the screen.

Fear and grief swallowed her, and she thought she might faint. Gone, how could they be gone?

"Lilly," Tray said softly as Dallas' voice prattled on and on in the background. "Lilly," he said again more firmly.

She looked at him and knew he was seeing into her soul, seeing her pain. She blinked and looked down at the table, she took a deep breath and felt his hand on her leg under the table. It was comforting and she managed to pull herself back from the edge. Nothing was certain, but everything she learned had her leaning more and more toward the worst-case scenario.

"How the hell does all of that fit into that small box?" she mused to distract herself as he held it up for her to see.

"It doesn't, not exactly," Patrick said. "I'm not sure how to really explain the internet to you."

"Georgia, go ahead, touch the screen and it will zoom to wherever you want, you could see whatever town you came from," Dallas said, handing her the device.

She took it and lightly touched a spot on the map, there was a sudden whooshing of the picture and it zoomed into an image of a completely unfamiliar plot of land full of houses and roads. Then she spotted the river she was pretty sure ran the length of her father's land. She touched it and again the image whooshed down to look like she was standing on a street along the bank. A street that her father never would have allowed to be built so close to pack land.

Not pack land anymore, Dallas said there was no pack in Georgia anymore. "Nothing about this looks familiar," she whispered, and tears stung her eyes.

"That's to be expected after so long," Tray said. He took the phone and passed it back to Dallas. "Don't worry about the past or what has changed. Think about the future," Tray said.

The future, she was living in the future, and she wasn't sure she liked it at all. "The pack isn't there anymore, they could have moved. But not my father, he never would have left home and the place I'd go back to if I ever got away. He would have stayed there waiting for me."

Tray put a comforting hand on her shoulder.

"I'll make some calls, see if anyone knows of him. You said his name was Roald Lancaster?" Patrick asked.

Lilly nodded. "That was the name he used with the pack, it was different for humans, changed over the years of course. But I believe that was his birth name."

"Packs keep good records; we'll figure it out."

"Thank you," she said.

"Dallas, clear the table," Patrick ordered then.

"I'll help," she said quickly and stood to start, she didn't mind at all. She actually enjoyed the human task and being useful, she knew that werewolf packs worked as a team. Everyone pitched in and had a job to do, no one sat around when there was work to be done and no one in need suffered without assistance. Her father had made sure that after she'd turned wolf she wasn't treated any different than any of the males in the pack. She learned to protect, hunt, and fight just like any other and all the males knew how to cook, clean and serve others. Gender roles were miniscule, although the humans among the pack were certainly treated with a different kind of respect, a certain gentleness and care. But it had less to do with their gender and more to do with the fact that they were so damn breakable.

"You're taking this all pretty well," Dallas said as they cleared the table. Tray and Patrick had disappeared outside.

"Is there another option?" she laughed.

"I guess not. I'm just glad we don't have to lock you up in the basement," Dallas said with a grin.

Lilly decided she liked Dallas; he was like a goofy big brother.

Tray walked in then and held up a flower he must have picked up outside. "Would you take a walk with me?" he asked.

Lilly blushed and dried off her hands, looking around at the still messy kitchen.

"Oh, don't worry about all that, I can clean up," Dallas said, leaving her with little choice but to accept Tray's offer of a walk.

Lilly took the daisy, and she twirled it in her fingers as she followed Tray outside. He offered his arm when she stepped off the porch. She grabbed onto it lightly and he led her toward a wooded area. He didn't speak until they were far enough away from the house that there was no chance of being overheard by Dallas or Patrick.

"Lilly, I would like to offer myself to you," Tray said.

"W—what?" she stammered, taken aback by the upfront offer, not that she didn't know what was in his head this whole time.

Tray stopped and moved to face her. He grabbed her hands and looked into her eyes. The desire she saw there lit a fire in her body, and she licked her lips, her gaze flicking down to his mouth.

He took that as an invitation and he leaned forward, pressing his lips to hers in a soft probing kiss. He didn't force entry, but when she parted her lips for him slightly, he dove in, taking the kiss to a deep passionate level. One hand went around to her back and pulled her against him. He groaned as her lower body rubbed his, already hard with desire. Everything about him was hard aside from his lips and tongue and she loved it.

She couldn't stop herself from responding, she didn't want to stop. It had been too long since she'd been caressed and kissed, too long since someone had looked at her and wanted her. She ran her hands up into his hair and held on as their tongues fought for control of the kiss.

He pulled back slightly and nipped at her bottom lip, then her jaw, and pressed kisses all the way up to her ear. His tongue flicked out and teased her lobe, then he whispered all the things he wanted to do to her right there on the forest floor.

And she was here for it, wanted him to make good on all of

those promises. She didn't give a shit about the consequences, she wanted to feel.

Her knees were weak, and she held onto him to keep from falling. His hands went to her ass and squeezed, lifting her enough that her feet floated an inch above the ground.

"Lilly, tell me yes. Let me have you," Tray groaned and bit gently at her neck.

"Yes," she gasped. How could she say no? This man was beautiful, passionate, and real. This wasn't a dream she'd awaken from to find herself still trapped in the body of her wolf, desperate for the touch of another human again. This wasn't a forced mating, an exercise in futility that would end up with heartache and abuse from captors.

"Oh Lilly," Tray groaned and dropped to his knees in front of her. His hands slid up under her skirt, quickly discovering that she wasn't wearing any underwear. He froze as his fingers touched the bare skin of her ass. He looked up into her eyes and his blue gaze darkened hungrily. A growl rippled from his chest that was more wolf than man and it made her tremble with anticipation.

Lilly parted her legs slightly in encouragement and he took it. He dipped his fingers between her thighs and began to caress and explore with gentle touches. Lilly still had her hands in his hair, and she threw her head back howling at the sky as he began to stoke the burning need in her body.

"I can't wait," Tray groaned and pulled her down. He positioned her with legs spread over his hips and he quickly wiggled himself free of his pants and underwear.

She reached between them and felt his hard length. She stroked him as she pressed her lips to his, licking and biting at his mouth until his hands were gripping her waist almost painfully. The growl from his chest was loud enough to be heard back at the house she was certain, and she didn't care.

They worked together to move her body and position his erection so she could sink down on him, knees digging into the dirt.

She loved that they were coming together in nature, raw and unhinged. It pleased the animal inside of her and she rocked her hips furiously as his finger played between them making her gasp and tremble.

"God, Lilly, I'm going to come already. Come with me," he groaned and stroked his finger against her faster until she was howling at the sky once again and he joined her, his howl dwarfing hers and going far enough to get an answer from a distant wolf.

Her body trembled with the waves of passion until she collapsed against his chest, a satisfied lump. His body trembled against and inside of her. His hands ran up and down her back in a soothing pattern. Their hearts began to slow, beating in time with each other, their inner wolves recognizing another of its kind and feeling satisfied.

That simple act of coming together had healed something inside her that she hadn't wanted to admit was broken and she felt tears sting her eyes as she breathed in the scent of their passion.

"I didn't mean for that to happen," Tray said after a few minutes of companionable silence.

"Oh," Lilly said, embarrassed. She moved off him, the pop of his member as it fell from her body a loud reminder of what they'd just done. She was obviously a horny mess and she had just jumped on him like he was the last steak on the table.

"Hey," Tray said softly and grabbed her hand. He easily pulled her back into his lap.

She sat sideways there, and he grabbed her chin to turn her face. He smiled and kissed the tip of her nose.

"I only meant to take you on a walk and declare that I intend to seduce you," he laughed. "I didn't expect that having you close to me would be so overwhelming. I couldn't stop myself from taking you out here like an animal."

"Oh," she said with a giggle. "I guess I was a little bit eager, it's been a while," she admitted.

Tray laughed. "I suppose it has." He kissed her softly. "I intend to seduce you many more times, and with longer results. Much more thoroughly and time consuming even," he said with a tinge of redness to his cheeks.

"It was perfect," she assured him and kissed his nose. There was a time and place for slow and this hadn't been it.

"I recognize that you are mine, Lilly. Can't you feel it?" he asked, desperation tinging his voice.

Lilly shook her head, hating that she was disappointing him. She didn't know what she felt for him, but letting another man claim her as his belonging wasn't something she was ready to do. Even if he was a werewolf with a big dick. "Tray, I don't think—"

"No," he cut her off. "Don't say anything, just know that I want you and I will do anything to keep you safe and make you happy."

She nodded, what else could she do after a declaration like that? She'd never felt so loved and cared for except with her own father.

They straightened their clothes and decided to take the intended walk. They talked of nothing important, keeping it light after an afternoon of heavy. When they returned to the house, the sun had set. The others were nowhere to be seen and it was a bit of a relief to not have to face them after they no doubt heard her and Tray's passionate howls earlier. Sex didn't embarrass her, but she wondered if she should worry about them thinking she'd accepted his claim on her.

Tray led her up the stairs to the bedroom and as soon as the door was closed, he scooped her into his arms and carried her to the bed. She decided she didn't care enough what the others thought, she just wanted more time feeling the way Tray made her feel.

He made love to her slowly and she felt his soul in it. He was showing her everything, nothing held back, and she nearly cried when it was over and he just held her tight, stroking her bare skin with his gentle fingers and whispering about the future. His fingers traced along the red scar lines and she didn't feel damaged under his gaze.

"I will kill him," Tray whispered.

"Me too," Lilly agreed.

"No one will ever harm you again, Lilly. I won't allow it."

She couldn't respond to that so she just kissed the arm that was wrapped around her and sighed heavily. Her heart ached with all that he was trying to give her, but her mind wasn't convinced, and she fell asleep without saying another word because she couldn't trust herself not to agree to be his just so she wouldn't hurt him.

Eleven

TRAY TIPTOED out of the bedroom, closed the door silently, then slipped down the stairs. He'd brought Lilly back to the house and made love to her again, slow and proper this time in a bed. She deserved to be treated like a princess, not a farm girl tryst. Though the way she'd responded to him with her knees in the dirt as he rocked his cock into her told him she liked sex raw and real, just like him. She was perfection, his wolf had known it as soon as he'd spotted her, and all doubts had flown out of his head as his ass had ground against a rock while her hips had rocked against him.

He was hardening again just remembering the way she'd howled at the sky, no shame, no worry of being found or heard, just experiencing it with him. It was everything he wanted in a woman, and she was all his, whether she was willing to admit it yet or not.

He was feeling very good about himself as he walked into Patrick's office.

Patrick sat behind a big desk looking annoyed. "You slept with her," Patrick accused.

"Of course I did. She is mine."

"She doesn't need you to complicate her life, Tray. She needs to figure out her life outside of that fucked up situation she was in for so long."

"No shit, and how do you think she can do that? She has no money, no driver's license, no social security number, no home, no pack, nothing! You know damn well her father is dead, that whole pack was wiped out by disease in the thirties along with half the U.S. packs. We are all she has. She won't be safe without us."

Patrick nodded. "I just confirmed it," he said pointing to the open laptop. "She wasn't listed as a pack member ever. I think he was hiding her from the start, not willing to let anyone know he had a female."

"Can't blame him, and best kept that way," Tray said, and Patrick nodded in agreement. "Where's Dallas? Does his loud-mouth know to keep it shut?"

"As soon as we heard you two howling in the woods he was off to town to find a willing woman for the night. He likes her, he won't endanger her."

Tray couldn't help a little satisfied smile. He had something that Dallas wanted, and his natural competitiveness liked that very much. "You weren't driven off," he said with a frown.

"My wife is too far away to get to for a quick tumble tonight," he grumbled.

Tray didn't envy Patrick that, but it was safest to keep wives and families far from the packhouse, far from monthly turns and the violence that they could become. He would never have that problem with Lilly and that knowledge made him want to run back upstairs and kiss her awake.

The Stone was supposed to change some of that for the others.

"We have another problem though. I called Julie and guess who answered," Patrick said.

Tray frowned.

"Jovi and his monster have control of the Descendants at the moment."

Tray dropped into the seat across the desk. That wasn't good news for the Descendants, and he cared because they're human, but also, they might have some books he really wanted sooner rather than later.

"No doubt he used the Descendants' Stone against them and is playing with them like dolls," Patrick spat. "I don't particularly care for the group, but no one deserves to be under the vampires' control."

"No one deserves to be under anyone else's control. What do you want to do?" Tray asked.

Patrick shook his head. "I don't know. I am waiting to hear back from Brody, he's been on watch and will be able to tell better what's going on over there. Until then we wait, it's not safe to go back to the city though, not with all of that going on. I won't risk a run-in with the monsters if we can help it. I want the vampires doing their job."

Tray agreed and relaxed. If they didn't go back to the city, they weren't putting Lilly in danger yet. He liked that very much. "I want a look at the books they have, I want to know if the Stone will allow Lilly to carry our child."

Patrick huffed and glared at him. "You need her agreement before you try anything like that," Patrick said with a sigh. "I don't run my pack that way, Tray, and I don't have the patience for your possessive shit right now."

"We need the Stone and the books before I worry about her agreement," Tray said, unwilling to think that Lilly wouldn't eagerly agree. "What's the word from Katherine?"

Patrick shook his head. "Brody says that Ian was released when Jovi took over. So no doubt he was right behind us when we left her in Miami. My guess is he dragged her down to Atlantis and we'll be lucky to hear from her ever again."

Tray hated to admit that he didn't blame the vampire for that move. But he didn't like that it took Katherine away from her promise.

"We are in a wait-and-see position. We are too smart to act

rashly so we see how things play out with Jovi and the Descendants. We won't stand by and let innocents be harmed, but this is a mess that Julie and Ian created. Ian should have stopped Jovi years ago and Julie needs to learn she isn't an island. She thinks she can call us in whenever she feels like it while pretending we are monsters too." Patrick shook his head in frustration.

"Fine, it will give me time to woo Lilly thoroughly," Tray said with a smile, then left the office confident that by the time they retrieved the books from the Descendants, Lilly would be his willing mate. He picked some flowers and put them in a vase before heading back up to the bedroom. He set them where she'd see them in the morning light, then tucked himself behind her in the bed. Holding her as they slept was as good as sex in his mind, more intimate even.

He breathed in her scent and closed his eyes, ignoring the demanding rise of his cock. He fell asleep listening to her steady breathing and knew that he wanted this every night for eternity.

Twelve

LILLY'S DREAMS were filled with terrible memories of captivity and control. She woke in the dark, a sweaty trembling mess and at first the arms locked around her only made her fight harder, panic more. The chains were back and this time they were around her arms too.

"Lilly, you are safe," Tray said gently, and she remembered where she was, and who was in the bed with her. She buried her face against his chest and cried until she fell back to sleep. He stroked her back gently the entire time, whispering words of assurance and never asking for an explanation.

When she woke again, the sun was streaming through the window and Tray was snoring at her side. She lay still, staring at him in the morning light. He was a beautiful man, a capable lover, and a protective wolf. He was everything she'd ever thought she might want in a mate, but the last thing she wanted right now was to be leashed by a mate. She just got her two feet back, she wanted to know that she could stand alone on them.

She thought of leaving, of running off and finding her way on her own. Surely, she could find some way. But then she thought of the world she'd glimpsed as Brandon had run her through the city in search of vampires. She thought of the sleek silver device that both Tray and Dallas had in their pockets. She thought of the fucking tampons that were apparently for her monthly bleed that she was still too afraid to try and figure out. The world wasn't what she'd known before. A hundred years of captivity, living as a wolf, meant she had no idea how this new world worked. She wouldn't even know where to begin among these humans and it terrified her.

Knowing that she couldn't do it alone made her angry and too anxious to stay in bed. She slipped away from Tray's warm embrace, pausing to smell the flowers that he must have brought in while she'd slept. He was the most thoughtful man she'd ever known. She smiled as she pulled on a robe then snuck to the door.

"Where do you think you're going?" Tray said sleepily.

"Bathroom," she replied and hurried out without looking back.

With the bathroom door closed and locked behind her, she leaned against the counter and stared at herself in the mirror. She was a strong fierce werewolf woman and years of captivity hadn't changed that. She just had to keep reminding herself of that fact when everything felt like it was too much. She could do anything, she reminded herself. She'd survived, and she would continue to survive. She wouldn't allow Tray to own her. She could start a new life with the help of another pack perhaps, one that didn't have a werewolf member who took one look at her and thought *mine*. She pictured Tray as he'd moved over her, his eyes locked with hers as he'd brought her so much pleasure. Was it just because it had been a while that she'd felt it so strongly? He wasn't *that* good. Surely she didn't feel anything more for him than she'd feel for any sweet-talking sexy werewolf who gave her a couple good orgasms. She had no reason to think he was anything special and she would leave him to find her own way with no regrets.

She ignored the little stab in her chest that the thought of leaving Tray gave her, but he was too much, too intense. In his mind she was already something that belonged to him. She couldn't belong to anyone ever again.

She took a shower, confident that she had a handle on her life.

When she left the bathroom, she could smell breakfast cooking downstairs and coffee. Her mouth watered at the thought of coffee.

"There you are," Tray said when she stepped back into the bedroom wrapped in a towel. "I missed you." He pulled her to him and kissed her enthusiastically. His hands slipped into her towel, and she pulled away, refusing to meet his gaze.

"I smell breakfast," she said softly.

Tray grunted and she moved quickly to get clothing. She didn't even look at what she grabbed, just held it tight and turned to leave the room again, thinking she would go to the bathroom to dress since he was obviously not making any move to leave the room. In fact he stood where she'd left him, completely nude, and when she dared a glance at his face, she saw a frown there.

"What did I do?" he whispered and the hurt in his voice broke her heart.

She bit her lip and fidgeted with the things in her hands. "This is all just a lot, Tray." Tears stung the backs of her eyes. "Do you have any idea what I—how long," she choked on emotion. "It's just a lot. You're a lot."

"Ha, I am perfectly enough," he said with a smug smile and crossed the distance. This time he didn't grab her and touch her, he simply stood close and gazed into her eyes. "I will be whatever you need. I want to surround you with my affection, I want to be with you every second of every day into eternity and I want to provide you every morsel and every drop you need to eat or drink. I want to do all the things with you." He sighed. "But I can under-stand if you need me to be a little less, um, intense, I guess. I can do that for you, you'll see."

"I need coffee," she said again, not really sure how to respond to that proclamation.

"Then I will deliver." He rushed from the room, not bothering to dress and the shout of disapproval from the men downstairs as he must have rushed into the kitchen with his dick swinging was enough to make her smile.

She dressed quickly while she was alone. Pulling on a pair of jean shorts and a white t-shirt. She wiggled her toes and dug through the bag for shoes.

"Black, or cream and sugar?" Tray asked, holding out two steaming cups.

"Cream and sugar, please," she said gratefully and took the cup he offered.

"Patrick made bacon and eggs. But you should also eat some raw meat to keep building back your strength. Dallas is on his way out to hunt now."

"You guys don't have to do all that," she said, uncomfortable. "I'm not part of the pack, I can hunt for myself."

"That's a minor detail, we will fix it soon enough."

Lilly sipped the coffee, trying to form the words to tell him that she had no intention of joining Patrick's pack at this point. But how could she do that without hurting Tray's feelings again. "Good coffee," she gushed as the wonderful liquid filled her with a familiar warmth and distracted her from the thought. "I think I missed coffee almost as much as fresh air."

A look of hatred and murder crossed Tray's face, but he pushed it away and smiled at her. "Wait till you taste Patrick's bacon." He offered her his arm, but she hesitated.

"Are you going to put clothes on?"

He glanced down at his body and grinned. "If I must," he said dramatically and pulled on the sweats she'd worn the day before.

She had to admit they made him look even more delicious. His defined abs on full display and expanse of tanned chest and wide shoulders. Not to mention the outline of his well-functioning manhood. She drank more coffee and tried to keep her eyes focused on his face but the grin he gave her told her he knew exactly how amazing he looked.

"I am going to need underwear and shoes," she said as they walked out of the room. "Dallas doesn't seem to have picked any up."

"Idiot, how could he not have thought of those," Patrick said with a shake of his head. "We can head into town after breakfast if you want, or if you're not comfortable with that. I'm sure we can send Dallas again."

Either way she was going to be that much more beholden to these men and that didn't sit very well with her. "No rush. I'm sure I'll be okay," she said as they entered the kitchen and Patrick's breakfast distracted them from any more conversation on the subject.

Thirteen

LILLY CLEANED UP BREAKFAST, insisting that she didn't need help because she wanted to pay back even in a small way, their kindness. Of course when it came to starting the dishwashing machine, she had to ask Tray for help, and he laughed as he told her how to add the soap and push the right buttons.

"Neat," she said as the machine started to whir. "So convenient!"

"The modern world is full of conveniences. Wait until you hear about the microwave oven and cable television," Dallas said from the living room, obviously eavesdropping.

"That sounds interesting," she called back, but she wasn't sure her voice hid all of her apprehension.

They moved to the living room then, where Patrick was sitting looking nervous, and for an alpha that really didn't bode well. Tray sat beside her on the couch and grabbed one of her hands in his. She was too worried to pull away, she let him try and offer comfort.

"Tell me," she demanded. "Whatever it is, just tell me."

"There was a disease that wiped out most of the werewolves in the U.S. The Georgia pack didn't make it. Your father didn't make it," Patrick said.

"Oh," Lilly said and dropped her gaze to her bare feet, her toes curling into the thick rug. She was really and truly alone, at the mercy of these men. Her options had been cut, her vague plan of finding anyone who might feel obligated to help her because of her father was dashed.

She gasped for a breath, suddenly her skin itched, and she had to run. She bolted from the house, shifting to wolf as soon as she hit the porch and ran.

She knew Tray followed, of course he followed. She could feel his presence close behind, could hear his footsteps and breathing, but he didn't overtake her, didn't try and stop her. She ran and ran. She hit a wide road with speeding vehicles that confused her eyes and she turned, running the other direction. She crested a hill and looked down on a huge expanse of houses and roads. She howled and took off in another direction, away from the humans. She came to a lake and watched briefly as boats sped, people splashed, and music blared. She took off in another direction and ran and ran. Nothing she saw did she recognize. Nothing was the same and she felt like a time traveler lost in a future where she never should have been, didn't want to be.

She didn't stop until she couldn't breathe, and her legs ached. She collapsed in a heap in the dirt and panted, hating that her full strength hadn't returned. She'd run for maybe two hours, but she should have been able to run without stopping for at least five.

Tray stood over her, breathing heavy but still obviously in control, he was strong and capable, everything a werewolf was meant to be. He watched over her and listened for danger as she lay helpless. She felt safe with him watching, knew that she could close her eyes and wait for her strength to return.

After a while she shifted to human and sat up. Tray shifted as well and kneeled in front of her.

"I'm sorry for your loss, Lilly."

A tear slid down her cheek. "I'm alone. I don't even know this world I'm in anymore. I feel so helpless. I can't take care of myself unless I stay wolf and live in the forest, that I know," she said miserably and looked off into the distance. The forest wasn't what it used to be. Would she be able to roam freely there or was it all covered in people? It wasn't what she wanted anyway though, she wanted the life, the human one and the wolf one, the pack and the family. Everything she'd had as a child and grew up envying.

"Lilly," Tray said and took her into his arms. He wrapped his warm body around her and held her so tight she almost complained. "Why won't you accept me. Let me care for you, I swear you will want for nothing. I will be a good mate, I know I will."

Her body shook as tears fell from her eyes.

"Damnit, why do you cry? Am I that terrible a choice?" Tray demanded after she settled.

Lilly laughed and pulled back enough to look up into his face. "Tray, you think you're offering me a solution but you're offering me another cage. Don't you see that? You want to own me, keep me? What if I want to be free? What if I don't want a mate and possible children? What if I want to just be another werewolf in a pack, running and hunting, protecting and living free?"

Tray blanked out his face. "Oh."

"I don't want to hurt you, but I don't want to belong to anyone right now."

"But I belong to you," Tray said and kissed her sweetly. "You own my heart, I am trapped in your cage of love, it's all I want, all I need. Lilly, I am yours."

His words sliced at her heart, she'd never seen such rawness in the eyes of another and she didn't know what to do with it. She pursed her lips and did the only thing she could think to stop him from continuing in that line of declarations. She pushed him down and slid over his body, she kissed and licked and nipped at his skin until he was growling and rolling them over. He loomed over her with a fierce need in his eyes matching her own. He thrust into her and howled up at the sky.

She grabbed desperately at his shoulders and rode the wave of pleasure he rocked through her body. Her back was pressed into the dirt and there was a rock under one ass cheek she knew was going to leave a nice bruise, but she didn't care. All that mattered in that moment was the way he filled her, the way his body fit her so perfectly, and how he used it to bring her pleasure. She scratched her nails down his chest and bit his lip as he kissed her. She felt feral, felt like her animal was crawling just under her skin and soaking in the pleasure just as much as she was. His hips pounded against hers and he grunted and groaned into her mouth.

As she felt the release building, she grabbed his ass cheeks, demanding more, demanding harder, deeper. She howled a release that he followed right behind, his head thrown back, his hands grasping her breasts almost painfully, but she loved it.

When they were both panting and sated, he rolled so she was laying on top of him. He kissed the top of her head and rubbed his hands up and down her back, discarding leaves and chunks of dirt and rock that had pebbled into her skin. "Yours," he whispered.

She didn't respond, what could she say? Her body thought it belonged to him and she was starting to think her mind was only a couple orgasms away from agreeing.

* * *

Tray led her back to the packhouse and his mind swirled. She responded to his body like a mate, she welcomed him and enjoyed him as much as he did her. But she held her heart back, he could feel it. How could he convince her that he wanted only to make the rest of her life the most wonderful experience possible?

When they arrived at the house it was getting late. They'd hunted on the way back, catching small things, rabbits, and squirrels. He could tell she was gaining back a lot of strength she'd been missing, and it made him happy. Two days of sun had affected her skin too and the sleep last night had taken care of the dark circles under her eyes. She'd always been beautiful to him, none of those outside things had mattered, but seeing her health improve made his fears for her physical safety settle.

When they arrived at the packhouse and Tray saw a familiar car in the driveway, he was annoyed but not surprised.

Lilly hesitated at the tree line, sniffing the air.

Tray shifted to human and put a hand on her back. "It's just Patrick's wife. He must have called her. She's human," he added as if it weren't obvious.

Just then the very pregnant woman in question walked out onto the porch and waved at them with a bright smile. She was a small and pretty woman. Maybe five-two and although rounded and heavy with child, still probably less than a hundred fifty pounds. She had long red hair and bright green eyes, pale freckled skin and a contagious laugh. She loved everyone in the pack and took it upon herself to care for them whenever possible.

He usually loved having her around, but the thought of her taking over the care of Lilly made him angry.

"Is that her?" Mary called, her voice full of all the expected excitement.

"She's shy," Tray explained, taking a step forward.

Lilly shifted to human and stood uncomfortably. "Hello," she called.

"Oh dear, look at you. You look like you took a roll through the mud, come in and shower. I brought some stuff for you and I'm making a pot roast for dinner." Mary turned to go back inside, and Patrick appeared in the doorway. He wouldn't allow anyone near his wife if they weren't a hundred percent in control.

Tray met his gaze and nodded, assuring him that Lilly was fine, safe to be around, and that they had resolved her worry for the moment.

Patrick turned and followed his wife inside.

"She's pregnant," Lilly said.

"Yes, it's Patrick's first and he's very nervous. I think it's why he's so desperate to find the Blood Moonstone. He doesn't want to be away from her when she gives birth."

Lilly nodded.

"We both could use a shower," he said, then leaned close to whisper. "Should we save water and shower together?"

Lilly gasped and pulled away slightly. "You're insatiable."

"Yes," he agreed.

They were naked as they walked to the house and Lilly stayed close to him. There was no way to completely shield herself from the eyes of the others as they made their way, and he knew she had to be used to the nakedness that came with shifting and being a part of a pack. But he liked that she was a little shy about it now. Liked that she thought to use him to feel safer in the situation. It was obvious to him that her instincts were to trust him, but there was something keeping her brain and heart from accepting it just yet. He knew he was chipping away at her doubts though, and if he was determined and patient, he would get there. No matter how long it took, she would be his happy mate.

Patrick was in the kitchen with Mary when they passed, the couple shared easy hugs and kisses that made Tray ache for that kind of closeness with Lilly. Patrick put a hand to Mary's huge belly and kissed her neck, making her giggle.

Tray put a possessive hand to Lilly's back and imagined them in a similar scene, it was so easy to imagine and that filled him with excitement.

"I put a bag of things in the bedroom," Mary called as they passed. "Girlie things, but we can go shopping too if she wants," Mary added.

"I can't pay her back," Lilly said as they topped the stairs. "I can't—" she said with a shake of her head.

"Stop doing that," Tray hissed.

"What?"

"Stop worrying about that shit. No one expects anything from you."

She stopped at the bedroom door and looked at him. "That's not true, Tray. You expect me to give myself over to you and have your babies."

"No I—"

"The Blood Moonstone could do that, and I saw the look you gave them down there. When Patrick touched her belly there was heavy coveting in your eyes."

Tray was speechless, he couldn't deny it, but he would never force Lilly into anything. "Who wouldn't want that closeness?" he said carefully.

Lilly just shook her head. "I think I'll shower alone." She grabbed the bag Mary had left for her and headed to the bathroom.

Tray was left to glare at the closed door.

Dallas walked out of a nearby bedroom and patted him on the shoulder. "I was jealous at first that she seemed to like you, but now... maybe I'm happy to head into town and find myself between the thighs of a human when I get horny."

Tray punched Dallas in the face and walked into the bedroom, Dallas' laughter floated after him as he slammed the door shut behind him.

Fourteen

LILLY SHOWERED; memories of touching Tray filled her as she watched the dirt flow down the drain. She wasn't convinced it wasn't just because she hadn't had sex in so long that she was so obsessed with his dick, but damn, he knew how to use it.

Did hearts and futures really have to get involved? Babies?

She touched her concave stomach and bit her lip. She'd given up on those kinds of dreams so long ago, she'd been disappointed too many times, had seen the disappointment in too many others' faces as blood flowed between her thighs. She wasn't sure she could handle hanging hope on a Stone that may not even exist.

Would Tray even want her if the Stone wasn't found, or if it was and it didn't work? Was she just a warm womb he thought he could fill? She deserved better than being someone's incubator.

She washed her short hair angrily then stepped out and scrubbed her body with the fluffy towel until her skin was pink. She opened the bag Mary had left her and sighed in relief when she saw underwear, some kind of stretchy bra, and shoes. Never send a man to shop for necessities for a woman. She had also brought some lotion and a little makeup. Lilly took her time, slathering her body and brushing out her hair, then slipping into a pair of stretchy shorts and a loose tank top. She didn't bother with makeup, had never been much for the stuff.

She felt good in her skin as she left the bathroom.

Tray was waiting there for her when she opened the door. He was showered and dressed in clean jeans and t-shirt. His hair was still damp, and his eyes lit up when he looked at her.

"You look beautiful," he said.

"Whatever Mary is cooking smells good," she replied.

He offered his arm, and she took it, letting him lead her down to the dining room. Mary was setting the table with Dallas' help while Patrick stirred something on the stove. Dallas had a red mark on his cheek that made Lilly think she hadn't misheard the skin against skin in the hallway earlier. She couldn't help a smile because it only added to the whole scene being one of family and familiarity, and it made Lilly's heart ache. There was love and disagreement, but they all worked together and they all cared about one another.

"Well, you two smell better," Mary teased when she noticed them. "Dinner's just about ready and I know you werewolves are always hungry, so I made lots." She rubbed her distended belly. "I think I've been giving even Patrick a run for his money on eating since I got pregnant," she said with a happy sigh. "I'll be glad when he comes out and I can get back into my jeans."

Patrick came up behind Mary, embracing her, his hands on her belly. He kissed her neck sweetly. "You are more beautiful than ever."

"Oh stop, you have to say that," Mary said, turning in his arms.

"No, I have to provide for you because I knocked you up. I say that because I mean it," Patrick teased.

"Oh, you," she laughed and smacked his chest lightly then pulled away and went back to the kitchen. Patrick watched her go with a possessive hunger in his eyes that reminded Lilly of the way Tray looked at her.

She didn't miss the way Tray and Dallas both watched Mary

with a protective eye, not in a sexual way, but in an intense brotherly way. Packs were like that. Once you were in, you were a part of it for everyone. Instant family, instant belonging. She had missed that so much for so long. It had been terrible to be ripped from her pack, thrown to a new one and to have them slowly taken away too until it was just her. For so long it was just her.

"I have to admit, Mary is better at picking out clothes," Dallas said with a laugh as he passed her with a big salad bowl.

"You did alright, though she did think of underwear and shoes," Lilly said with a laugh.

"Oh, yeah, I don't wear underwear, so I guess I didn't think of that," Dallas admitted.

Tray rolled his eyes and Mary laughed in the kitchen.

"Dallas is the pack slut, but we love him despite his tendency to break hearts," Mary explained.

"You wound me, Mary. I provide orgasms and leave women with the memory of being completely satisfied. That can't be a bad thing."

"No, it's not," Lilly agreed with a laugh that earned her a hard look from Tray. She just shrugged. She was too old and had been through too much, to think that finding a way to be happy that didn't hurt anyone was bad.

And that's exactly what Tray was trying to do, wasn't it? She eyed him as he set out forks and napkins on the table. She couldn't blame him for grasping at happiness where he could. She was a little ashamed to admit to herself that she didn't know his story, had no idea what his past held. He could be covering a lot of pain with this obsessive desire to possess her.

Wow, she realized, she had been a bit of a selfish bitch. But who could blame her, she had just escaped a hundred years of captivity.

Dinner was full of conversation, and she listened intently as Mary relayed news of other werewolf wives and their children. It sounded to Lilly like Patrick had a large pack and most of them had significant others and many with more than one child. The picture it created in her mind was comforting and familiar. As far as she'd always known, all packs were this way. Family-oriented and kind. They cared for each other and each other's families. They worked to make the world in general a better place, safer for humans obviously, but also protective of nature.

"What do you all do for work?" she asked when there was a lull in the conversation.

"I inherited some property from my father," Patrick said. "It runs itself really, farmland. I just make the big decisions when needed but mostly take care of pack business."

"Much to my father's disappointment, I opened a little bar in town," Dallas said with a grin.

"More like a strip club," Mary said with a laugh.

"They don't strip, they just dance."

"With barely anything on," Mary added.

Dallas grinned. "It's good money and I make sure the girls are safe. Better they work at my place than the other options for girls in that position. No one gets handsy in my clubs and no one has to do anything they don't feel comfortable with."

Lilly didn't comment, it sounded reasonable and it did seem like Mary was only teasing him.

"Does your father still disapprove?" she asked Dallas.

"He stopped disapproving before he passed." A sadness passed over Dallas' features but quickly left, covered again by his usual boyish grin.

"What about you?" she asked Tray.

"I work for Patrick."

"You're his beta?" How had she not seen that already? Tray was obviously a powerful werewolf, could probably be an alpha himself if he wanted.

"Something like that. I keep peace. I make sure no one steps out of line."

"Do they?" she asked.

"No, my job is boring," he confirmed.

When dinner was done, the men retreated to Patrick's office and Lilly helped Mary clean up.

"Tray is a nice guy," Mary said slyly. "He doesn't date a lot, just so you know, not like Dallas. I think he's been holding out for the one."

"We aren't dating," Lilly said quickly.

"No? Are you sure he knows that?" she laughed.

Lilly frowned as she carried plates from the table to the kitchen. "I told him I don't intend to belong to him."

"Oh honey, our hearts choose who they belong to, not our minds. Do you think I would have chosen a werewolf if I'd had a choice?"

Lilly gave her a curious look. "You didn't know when you met Patrick?"

"I had no idea! I just saw the big sexy thing across the bar and strode over and asked for a dance," Mary said with a smile.

"Bold move."

"Oh yes, I was never one to wait for a guy to approach me, I always go after what I want. We danced all night, and I took him home with me."

Lilly liked Mary a little bit more for that. Here was a woman who made things happen for herself, she wasn't a pushover and as the mate of a very dominant werewolf, that was a good thing. "How long until you found out?"

"Well, we were inseparable for two weeks." Mary paused, her cheeks reddened, and her lips curved up into a smile as she no doubt remembered nights and days filled with passion with her newly discovered man. Mary cleared her throat and snapped back to the present. "And then he made up a stupid excuse to leave for the full moon." She shook her head and dropped a plate into the sink with more force than necessary. "I was certain he was done with me and just blowing me off for another girl, maybe a wife or something crazy. He was just too good to be true; polite, handsome, great in the sack, and rich. He treated me like the most precious thing he'd ever encountered, and it was magical for those two weeks."

"So what did you do?"

"Like a true crazy woman, I followed him. I figured I would out him to whoever he was meeting up with. If he was going to screw women over, he deserved to be confronted and lose both of us. I thought I was pretty sneaky, but of course he knew I was following. He's a werewolf so his senses are great, obviously and my car was pretty obvious on some of the roads he was taking. I still figured I was stealth though because when he stopped a couple times for gas and to take a piss, he never glanced back to where I'd parked along the side of the road. He was allowing me to follow, he was leading me the whole time. I was following him right into a trap." She shook her head and smiled at the memory. "He stopped at this little motel about an hour from here and checked in. I thought I would catch him in the act, confront him and break up with him. I waited two hours after he went into the room and although I didn't see anyone with him, I figured the other woman must have already been in there, so I knocked on the door and he answered with a huge smile. I yelled and yelled and called him every name in the book. He just took it, didn't say anything until I was done. Then I looked around the empty room and demanded to know where she was. I even checked the bathroom and under the bed as if his wife or longtime girlfriend would have nicely hidden from me while I screamed at him for cheating. Then he sat me down and explained everything. I didn't believe him of course so he showed me, shifted right there in the hotel room. I screamed and ran out, drove home, and tried to convince myself that it had all been a hallucination. That I'd actually walked in on him with some other woman and my mind made up the werewolf story to ease the pain."

"Wow, I can't imagine what that must have felt like. I grew up knowing. I never went through a finding out. The closest thing for me was finding out that not everyone turned into a wolf once a month. Let me tell you, I was pissed at three when my parents told me I would never be able to do that." Lilly smiled. "They were wrong, obviously."

"It would seem so," Mary laughed.

"So what happened next?" Lilly asked, completely invested in Mary's story.

"He showed up two days later with flowers, chocolates and a stuffed wolf toy." She shrugged. "I didn't care what he was, I just wanted to keep feeling the way he made me feel. If he had to wolf out once a month, no big deal, at least he was faithful."

"Sounds like a true love story."

"It is," she agreed. "Can I ask you something?"

"Of course."

"Have you ever regretted becoming one?"

"So many times," Lilly admitted. "When I found out I would never be able to have children, when I was captured by the Aristotle Society and nearly every day I spent locked in a cell."

"Do you still regret it?" Mary asked quietly.

Lilly thought it over and realized she didn't. She wouldn't give up her power for anything. "No."

"Even though you can't have a child?"

"Patrick thinks the Stone might change that." Did she hope it would? She wasn't sure.

Mary's eyes lit up with joy. "Would you try? With Tray? Oh, he would be the best father; I just know it. The way he is with his packmates' kids, he has the touch, you know. Sometimes you can just tell a guy knows how to be a father. And you two would make the most beautiful babies," she squealed.

Lilly busied herself rinsing dishes and avoided Mary's eyes. "I don't know, but having the option might be nice, someday." She shrugged. Options were always good, something she hadn't had for too long. "I don't really know where I fit right now to be honest. I'm not sure I'll be staying in Patrick's pack. I might see if any of my father's pack survived the disease, though it seems doubtful." She had to admit she didn't really care about that anymore. It wasn't her father so what did it matter?

Mary let out a horrified gasp. "You can't be thinking of joining with Weston? He's nasty, oh man, his men are nasty and the one time Patrick let them come into his territory they nearly killed that poor Descendant girl."

"Weston?"

"Yeah, he's the only other pack leader left in the U.S., unless you plan to go rogue, but that has its own dangers." Mary talked fast as she packed away leftovers and frowned with worry.

This woman was a fount of information Lilly realized. What else had Tray and Patrick not told her? "How much land does Patrick control?"

"Everything from the east coast to the Mississippi river. Weston controls everything west of that. There are some pods here and there controlled by local beta wolves, but Patrick and Weston are the biggies I guess you'd say."

"Because of the virus? Only two alphas survived?"

Mary nodded. "I wasn't around then of course, but they still talk about it, lost a lot of friends. Entire lines of werewolves were taken down."

"It must have been hard." Lilly wasn't sure how she felt. Was it better to have missed that? She probably would have died along with the rest of her pack, but she would have avoided so much pain at the hands of the Aristotle Society. And now she was alone. Her eyes drifted to the closed office door where Tray had gone. She was only alone if she wanted to be, she had to admit. There was Tray who wanted to be her mate, Patrick who wanted to be her alpha, and Mary. She looked at the woman who was humming as she wiped the counter. Mary wanted to be her friend.

"Tray was lucky. His entire pack up near Canada died but somehow, he made it through. Seemed like the virus chose him special," Mary continued.

"He didn't originate in Patrick's pack?"

"Oh no, he came to us a few years ago. He'd been rogue for a long time after his pack died. He's the one who came across the wolves from Weston's pack who had a Descendant girl out in the woods. He attacked, distracting them long enough for the girl to pull out her weapon and fight back as well. A vamp swooped in and got the girl out. In the end it was just one living wolf that Tray dragged back here to confront Patrick with. Tray wanted to make sure that Patrick wasn't running his pack like that and when he found out that Patrick definitely wasn't, he decided to stay for a bit. When he joined, I think he hadn't been in human form for years by the way he acted. Some of the other wives were a bit afraid at first, but the way he took to the children so quickly, it was telling. I could see the strong good man under the rough exterior, and I was right, because now he's a favorite. Wives are always trying to set him up with their friends and the kids go crazy when *Uncle Tray* comes around," Mary laughed. "Boy will there be some disappointed girls when they hear about you."

Lilly blushed; she didn't know how to respond so she didn't. It gave her a lot to think about though and she wondered even more about Tray's past. What had he been running from in wolf form?

Fifteen

TRAY PACED in Patrick's office as he listened to the conversation coming out of the phone. Brody was the scout watching the Descendants' place and he was reporting chaos inside. Jovi had shown up with Norgis after they evacuated the place.

"Where the hell is Ian?" Patrick growled.

"No sign of him, Boss, but by the show that Jovi is putting together, I am guessing he expects his brother to arrive tonight. He better bring help. We are standing watch and we will go in if necessary to stop unnecessary bloodshed," Brody said. "Just waiting for your word."

"Maybe we should be there," Dallas said. "That monster needs to be contained."

"Yes, it does, but it's not our job," Patrick mumbled.

"What is our job if not defending the human population?" Tray growled. "I didn't join your pack to sit around and watch television, Patrick. We've been the line of defense between the vamps and humans for centuries."

"And the vamps are supposed to stand between the monsters

and the humans," Patrick pointed out. "This is their mess. Ian needs to take care of it."

"Ian's not there, his brother let him out and he scrambled off," Tray snapped.

"To get his woman, are you saying you'd do anything different?" Patrick snapped back.

Tray clenched his jaw because it was true. He'd have gone after Lilly too, if she'd been taken by the vamps the way they'd taken Katherine. "That doesn't mean he's coming back to finish the job," Tray said quietly.

Patrick sighed. "We'll be there in a few hours," he said and hung up the phone. "We go and watch, we give Ian twenty-four hours to fix this, or we go in. I won't let Jovi have a foothold in my territory, especially not with a monster like Norgis."

Tray smiled, anticipating a fight. "Great, and in thanks they can give us any books they have on our history and the Stone."

Patrick agreed and met Tray's gaze across the table. That Stone could change everything.

"When do you want to leave?"

"Give me an hour with Mary and I'll send her back. I don't want her out here by herself."

"We'll be ready," Tray grunted and left the office. He found Lilly in the kitchen with Mary chattering on and on about the members of the pack. That woman loved to talk.

"Mary, Patrick wants you in his office," Tray said.

"Oh, okay," she said happily and as she passed Tray, she pulled his head down to kiss his cheek softly and whisper her approval of Lilly.

"She's a sweet girl, don't hurt her."

Tray couldn't imagine hurting her and he assured Mary he wouldn't. Lilly was finishing up in the kitchen and he pitched in to help and told her the plan.

"Is it dangerous?"

"Shouldn't be, unless Ian doesn't do his job," Tray said. "We have an hour."

"I guess I'll pack the things upstairs," she gave a nervous laugh. "I don't want to leave it behind, it's not as if I can just replace it."

Tray frowned, he wanted so badly to reassure her, but it wouldn't do any good. He had to show her that she could be happy relying on him. That the only thing he wanted for the rest of forever was to take care of her in every way, anywhere that she wanted. He hadn't had a permanent residence in a long time so he was flexible, maybe she'd want to settle in her familiar territory of Georgia to remind her of her father. Maybe she'd want to be far from those memories. She deserved to have a place to call home somewhere, a place to settle and heal from old wounds.

He wanted to give that to her. The fact that she was nervous about leaving anything here that she could almost call her own made him angry and sad.

"Go ahead, I'll finish this up," Tray said. He watched her walk away and was transported back to another time, another pack-house and another woman who had walked away from him.

He'd told her what he was, had revealed himself to her and she'd turned away from him, throwing hateful words over her shoulder. *I won't be married to a monster, Tray. I won't raise children with a man-eating beast. How could you do this to me?* Larissa's words had ripped his soul apart because he couldn't deny them. He was a monster; a beast and he always would be. She was better off without him, she could have a real future with a human the way she never could with him.

Two months later he'd caught a glimpse of her walking down the street on the arm of a man, a human man, and with an obvious new bulge to her belly. A rage like nothing he'd ever felt filled him. She was pregnant with his child and she had likely known it when she'd left him that day. She obviously had no intention of ever telling him. She had a ring on her finger and the man beside her smiled down at her like she was the moon and stars.

He'd followed her for two days before catching her alone one evening and confronted her. She admitted she was carrying his child but it didn't matter to her. As far as anyone would know, it was Peter's child, and she was already married to him anyway.

This child will never know what kind of horrific monster its father is. If you come around me again, I swear to god I'll kill it rather than let you drag it into the hell of your existence.

He'd stayed away because he believed her words as she'd held a knife to her own belly, facing him across her kitchen. It had been painful, but he'd watched his son grow up from afar. Saw him get married and start a family of his own. He'd watched his son die of old age surrounded by grandchildren and be buried next to his late wife. He'd watched so many people mourn the loss of such a great man who'd led an amazing life. A life that Tray hadn't been allowed to be a part of.

He'd felt every bit the monster that Larissa had thought he was, until he'd seen Lilly.

The heart that could feel such soul-encompassing love for another couldn't be held within a monster, and he knew that if he could get Lilly to love him in return, it would prove Larissa had been wrong. It would prove that he wasn't ruined because he'd been turned into this thing. None of them were. Werewolves could be good or bad, same as humans, and they deserved love and a life and family, same as humans.

A monster was created through choice, not circumstance.

Even the vampires weren't all bad.

But every time Lilly denied him her heart, every time she frowned and walked away, it was like Larissa was laughing in his head. Telling him that a monster like him would never find happiness. The curse of a werewolf was to kill the ones they loved the most. Larissa had been smart to stay away, to keep his son away, and Lilly would never give herself over to him and risk a child with him. Lilly was too smart to make that mistake.

He wanted to rage, to kill, and he hoped he'd get the chance to sink his teeth into a deserving vampire. For now he'd settle for a rabbit or small deer though and he left the cabin with a growl.

Sixteen

BRODY HUNG up with Patrick and made another call.

"Yes, what good news do you have for me?" The deep voice answered.

"There is chaos at the Descendants' compound and the vampires are in the mix," Brody explained quickly. "Patrick's keeping the pack out of it as best as he can, he trusts the vampires for the most part. But they are on their way here to make sure the monster is taken back to its watery prison."

"And the Stone?"

"Still hasn't been located."

"Keep me updated, I can't wait to bring you into the pack under me, Brody, you're proving yourself useful."

"I look forward to it," Brody said, and the line went dead.

He didn't have a single tinge of guilt over his decision. Not when Patrick insisted on keeping him so low in the pack. Patrick wouldn't have ordered one of his favorites to sit out here and watch, oh no, they got to go with him to Miami, got to spend time at the packhouse outside of the full moon and carouse in the nearby small town where there were always willing women at the bar.

Patrick and his entire pack would regret the decision to not respect Brody's potential.

Brody positioned himself with a clear view of the front entrance. The screams had mostly stopped, and he supposed that meant the Descendants' Stone was in use in there, keeping them calm as they were fed on, and who knew what else.

Did vampires fuck their meals? They used to be human, so Brody supposed they probably did. Unless their lust had died, leaving behind only the bloodlust. He'd hate a life like that, sex was the only good thing about his life sometimes. He had a crappy job on one of Patrick's farms and he lived in a small-ass apartment surrounded by humans. He couldn't afford a house, and unless he got married and added to the pack numbers, Patrick wouldn't give him a significant raise. He claimed the married werewolves needed it more, but Tray and Dallas were never short on funds, Brody knew that.

But he was on his way up. Soon he'd be living his best life on the west coast with sunshine and beach babes everywhere. He could almost howl just thinking about it.

Seventeen

LILLY GATHERED the things that had been given to her and stuffed them in an empty shopping bag. It wasn't much, but it was all she could claim as her own and that thought was depressing as hell.

She didn't know what was to come next for her. Didn't know if she'd be back here or if she even wanted to be. But she did know she couldn't afford to leave behind anything at this point. She would be left to steal anything she needed without Patrick's pack, and she really didn't like that thought. She'd grown up wanting for nothing. Her father had been wealthy, and he had taken very good care of her. She had never even considered needing a job, which looking back seemed ridiculous. Her father had thought she'd just marry and live the life of a mother and wife for eternity. Now she wondered if she was even qualified for anything. Probably not. Unless she learned a hell of a lot about the world first anyway. She was helpless to find work outside of selling her body on the street corner.

Frustration filled her and she threw the bag onto the bed then walked out onto the little balcony. She saw a flash of red fur, Tray was running, hunting maybe. She wondered if he would bring her back some fresh meat, then chastised herself for the thought. He didn't have any obligation to take care of her, even if he did continue to act like it. She shouldn't get used to it, shouldn't accept too much and let him overthink their time together. After they killed Brandon, she was going to get on with her life, whatever that was. *Tray is just a fling*, she told herself firmly.

So then why did the thought of their time coming to an end feel so heart-wrenching?

"He really is a good guy," Dallas said, startling her and making her turn around.

"Yeah, seems great," she said carefully.

"I don't know his whole story," Dallas added. "I'm sure Mary told you everything she knows. That woman loves to talk. I think he's been a werewolf for a very long time and that does something to a person. I guess you know that too. Just don't judge him harsh because he wants a bit of normal." Dallas shrugged.

Normal, did she even know what that was anymore? For the last hundred years her normal had been four furry paws and a collar around her neck. She'd never had human normal because she'd grown up in a pack. So what was normal for a couple of werewolves?

This, she had to admit. A pack, an alpha, safety, and family. This was normal for a werewolf. Tray just saw in her a way to make that normal a little bit better for himself. She couldn't blame him for wanting that.

"Patrick would never put you in a situation you didn't want to be in," Dallas continued. "If you want out, if you need to be away from Tray and his intensity, just tell him. None of us want to see you on your own, it's dangerous. Just let him know what you need. You can have a place in this pack that doesn't include Tray if that's what you're worried about."

She sighed heavily and turned back to stare out at the night. Did she want to be away from Tray? She wondered where he'd run off to. She admitted she wanted to be with him right now, was a little offended he hadn't asked her to go on a run with him. She supposed it was her own fault though, she kept pushing him away, so of course he went away. A clear sign that he was trying to be patient and give her room to breathe and figure things out.

Why did he have to keep doing the perfect gentlemanly thing? It made her like him more. Not that she could tell him that, he'd put a ring on her finger before she had time to say *slow down*.

Lilly walked back to the bed and laid down to rest until it was time to leave. The scent of Tray puffed up from the bedding and made her smile.

It wasn't long before she heard a soft moan and answering growl from a nearby room, and she knew that Patrick was making love to his wife before sending her back. Lilly couldn't help wondering what that must be like. To be so protected and so loved. To be carrying a child and know that you were building a life with someone.

Tray wanted to give that to her because he wanted it for himself. But what if she couldn't give it to him? What if, even with the Stone, it didn't work? Would he reject her then, like the others had? Could she handle the promise of having everything, only to end up alone again?

Had her father tried to warn her of this? Was that why he'd hesitated so hard when she'd asked to be turned?

"You won't be able to live a full life," he'd said.

"A full life? I'll live forever without aging! How can that not be a full life?" she'd scoffed.

"You don't know what you're giving up, you're too young to know the sacrifice you are making."

"I'm twenty-two, if I get much older, I'll start to disintegrate and you'll look younger than me," she snapped. "I don't want to be older than my father."

"I don't want to take life from you. Why not just marry and have a family? You can live forever through your children and grandchildren."

"Why is that my only option? Because I'm female?" she'd demanded and the look of chagrin on his face told her it was exactly that. "I want this, so if you won't do it, I'll find someone else who will."

And he hadn't been able to deny her, had never been able to deny her anything she'd really wanted.

"It's not proper for a father to outlive his children," she'd added just to stick her point home in his heart.

"No, it's not proper," he'd agreed.

Lilly frowned at the memory, she had outlived him, but did he know that? He'd probably mourned her when she'd been captured, probably thought she'd died then. The silver collar had cut off her ties to the pack as if in death. If he'd felt that, had he instantly given up hope, or had he wondered and searched. Had he had even an inkling of an idea that the Society had been behind it. She liked to think he was watching her now from the embrace of death though. That he now knew what had happened and that she'd survived.

"I will keep surviving, Father. I will keep making something of my life," she whispered and wiped a tear from her cheek. "I don't regret what I am. I only regret believing I could do it alone that night."

Was she making the same mistake now? Convinced that she was capable enough to do it all on her own but about to walk into a trap? She felt like Tray was trying to cage her, but at the same time she could admit he was offering her safety and family and everything she had ever wanted.

Why did she feel like all her dreams coming true was a new sort of cage she was being shoved into? She didn't have an answer.

She was too anxious to rest now so she got up from the bed and walked across the bedroom to the open balcony doors to stare into the night. Two bright eyes stared up at her from the line of the woods and she knew Tray was there, watching her. She gave him a small wave and then turned to go back inside. She didn't have an answer for the question in his gaze, but she wanted to find one.

She paced the bedroom and let her mind flow through everything her life had been and the possibilities of what it could become. Somewhere in there was a decision that she needed to make.

An hour later they were saying goodbye to Mary who was all smiles as she got in her car to drive home. Then they piled into Patrick's car and headed toward the Descendants' compound and hopefully some valuable information.

* * *

Tray held himself back during the drive. He didn't touch her, and he didn't engage her in any more than surface level conversation. It was difficult. He wanted to pull her against him, he wanted to kiss her and tell her about the future he saw for them. He wanted to demand that she agree, wanted her to admit that she was his, forever and always his to take care of, to worship and build a life around.

He knew it wouldn't work; she wouldn't be pushed into anything. She was a strong woman, a strong wolf and she had to come to a conclusion in her own time. She'd already accepted him physically; she just wasn't ready to accept him mentally and emotionally. She would though, he was certain, because the alternative was too heartbreaking.

Patrick watched them carefully, ready to jump in if he got out of line which was another reason he held himself back. Tray couldn't risk a confrontation that would end with him killing Patrick or being banished from the pack.

When they arrived at the Descendants' compound it was all over. The Descendants were back in control and although the stink of vampire and monsters was heavy in the air, it was fading. Tray was thankful they hadn't been here for the fight. He didn't want

Lilly involved in anything that could get her hurt. She wasn't back to full strength yet and he had a feeling that wouldn't stop her from attacking a vampire or monster.

"This is a good thing, right?" Lilly asked as they stepped out of the car, and all came to the same conclusion.

"I think it is," Patrick said. "I would like to trust the vampires to take care of their duties."

Tray agreed it would be preferable if they could work together rather than against each other. It was hard to erase so many centuries of death though. So many years of werewolves killing vampires to keep humans safe. Most of that had been before Tray's time. As far as he knew, there hadn't been any large clashes since Ian had taken over for his father. Tray didn't know a lot about Ian's father, but he had heard that the man or vampire rather, had pissed off a witch once upon a time and of course, had been fine with enslaving the Descendants and taking them down with Atlantis as blood slaves.

Ian seemed to be a little more reasonable, if the lack of confrontations was any indication.

"Do you smell that?" Dallas said as they walked toward the wall surrounding the place.

"I smell blood and dead fish," Lilly said with a frown.

Dallas shook his head. "One of the vamps didn't leave the area. Someone's keeping watch."

"Not our problem," Patrick said and led the group forward.

Tray agreed and assumed it was Samson keeping watch over his woman, but just in case, he made sure to stay in step with Lilly, protective.

The quiet as they approached the once invisible gate was eerie. The last time they were here there'd been a lot of celebration for the capture of the vamps. Lilly didn't seem to mind him walking protectively beside her so he put a possessive hand to her back, thankful that she didn't pull away.

"Hey!" A voice called and Tray growled as Brody rushed to

their side. "Patrick, glad you're here, and you brought..." his voice trailed off as he looked Lilly up and down. Tray saw Brody's nostrils flare as he scented her, and his eyes widen as realization hit. "Oh my fucking god, is that a female werewolf?" Brody practically groaned.

Tray pulled her behind him, baring his teeth at Brody in a fierce snarl. "Get out of here," Tray snapped.

Brody put his hands up, taking a step back. "I—I didn't mean anything," he darted his eyes to Patrick who was currently glaring at Tray.

"No, you didn't, you were just surprised. This is my fault, I thought it best to keep her hidden for the moment, but I think the surprise might be too much," Patrick said reasonably.

It didn't calm Tray, however. He was ready to grab Lilly and run off, hide with her, and never let another male anywhere near her. She was his.

"Fuck yeah it's a surprise," Brody whispered, hands still up in a show of peace. "Where did you get her?"

"She's mine," Tray snarled.

"No, I'm not," Lilly whispered behind him, but the way she clung to his shirt told another story.

Patrick just shook his head. "Tell the others, we rescued her from what I hope is the last surviving member of the Aristotle Society. Warn them, he's still out there in Miami and he's untrained, dangerous. She is under my protection until she chooses to leave," he added the last with a harsh look at Tray.

"Like I have anywhere to go," Lilly said so quietly Tray was sure no one had heard it but him.

"I'll spread the word," Brody assured Patrick.

"You can leave your post here too. We are here to see what Julie knows about the Stone, then we're heading to Miami to kill a man."

Brody smiled broadly. "I'll stick around for that!"

"No," Patrick said. "I don't think a bigger pack is what will do the trick. I don't want to risk losing more wolves to him if he's not as untrained as I think. Just tell the others what we're doing. The guy's name is Brandon, owns some pawn shop downtown Miami. We plan to kill him quickly, but just in case, the others should know." Patrick took a deep breath. "And send someone to sit with Mary until I get back."

"Will do," Brody said and dared to lean around so he could see Lilly behind Tray's back. "It was nice to meet you. I hope you decide to stay in the pack."

Tray felt her nod behind him, and his chest rumbled. He didn't like the way Brody's eyes lit up as he gazed at her.

"My name is Lilly," she said. "My father was alpha of the Georgia pack."

"I'm sorry," Brody said with real pain in his eyes. Brody was an old wolf and he'd been around when the sickness had wiped out so many.

"Was Katherine with the vampires when they came?" Patrick asked, thankfully taking the focus off Lilly.

"Yeah, she was here with Ian, and they took off again together with some beasts from Atlantis. Jovi is dead, thank god, and the Descendants have been quiet the last few hours."

"There's a vamp still in the area," Dallas pointed out.

"Yeah, the big one is watching. He scented me but doesn't seem to care about my presence. He'll be finding a place to hide for the night soon, I'm sure."

"Samson," Tray said, now sure.

They turned their gaze back to the building. It worried Tray that no one had come out to question them as they'd stood there talking and he looked up at the large house. There was at least one Descendant watching through a window. He saw a red head there peering out. He recognized that red hair and he gave a little wave.

She didn't respond, he knew she didn't trust them. He didn't blame her; he'd seen what happened to her before he got there.

"Let's go in so we can get back out," Tray said, anxious to be away and let these people heal in peace.

He wrapped an arm around Lilly's back, guiding her down the driveway and up the steps. Patrick and Dallas followed while Brody melted back the way he'd come, no doubt already on the phone spreading the news of Lilly.

Tray didn't like the idea of everyone knowing about her, but Patrick wasn't wrong, the surprise was worse.

Patrick banged on the door and unsurprisingly Chase was the one to answer. He was the second in command under Julie, who was Sorcha's sister. Tray didn't trust her, anyone who would lock up her own sister the way she had wasn't someone that would hesitate to turn on a business deal.

"What the hell do you want?" Chase demanded. He had a fierce look on his face and a weapon in his hand. Nothing that would stop them, but a fight wasn't what they were after.

"We need to speak with Julie about some books," Patrick insisted and stepped forward, one foot over the threshold.

"I think you've gotten enough from us, dog," Chase snapped.

"Back off, Chase," Julie called from behind him. "What can they do that Jovi hasn't already done?"

Chase glared harder, but he moved out of the way. Tray kept one arm on Lilly and his eyes on Chase as they entered the foyer.

"Julie, it's nice to see you survived," Patrick said with a grin. He would put on a show of not caring, a show of power, and play the game because that's what Julie needed in order to know that she couldn't walk all over them. Tray knew it killed Patrick to see them harmed, same as any other human, but they didn't respect the wolves any more than they respected the vampires. Julie was willing to use them as a weapon though, without hesitation.

"Of course I survived, we almost all did," she said with a slight hitch to her voice. "And now we have possession of the Stone so no vampire can use it against us again."

"Wonderful," Patrick said magnanimously.

"What do you want?" Julie demanded.

"Books. What do you have on the Aristotle Society and the werewolves?"

"History?" she said with a frown, crossing her arms over her chest. She took up a power stance and matched Patrick for glares.

"Our history, and we intend to have it," Patrick said, letting a growl flow into his voice.

"What are you hoping to find? A way to make your girlfriend into a monster so you can fuck her without killing her?" Julie sneered, motioning to Lilly.

Lilly bared her teeth at the woman and let out her own growl. Julie's eyes widened in surprise.

"Well, I see you already got that far."

"Books," Patrick demanded, done with the chatter. He pushed past her and walked toward her office. "I know they are in here; I saw them."

Julie stormed after him, Chase hot on her heels to support.

Tray looked at Dallas, motioning with a quick nod that he should stay and watch the door. Then he pushed Lilly toward Julie's office.

Julie stormed past Patrick and went to the wall of books and started pulling things from the shelf. "Take them. Take whatever you want because apparently, we don't matter! We were the history keepers; we were the ones of reason and knowledge. We kept what was real and true and decided what humans should know, we protected them all!" Julie was yelling now, and Chase put a comforting hand on her shoulder.

She punched him.

"I don't care anymore! My own sister betrayed me and wants to leave me. My people were murdered. Our spells are down, and the witches won't help."

Tray wasn't sure what to do, the mental breakdown he was witnessing made him uncomfortable and he couldn't wait to get out of there, but they needed the books.

"Take what's yours," Chase said softly and pulled her gently from the room. "Then get out," he added as Julie sobbed against him.

Patrick looked dumbstruck and he met Tray's eyes for a moment before he started gathering the thrown books.

"Why don't you scan the titles on the shelves, see if there's anything else there that we should take," Tray instructed Lilly, then went to help Patrick pick up the books on the floor. They were old and dusty, and Tray wondered how long it would take to find anything useful in them.

Eighteen

LILLY RAN a hand over the dusty books and stopped at one that caught her attention. *Witches and Wolves,* it said. She pulled it down and heard a thump at her feet. She bent and picked up a silver bookmark. She knew it was pure silver, it scorched her hand, and she hissed as she set it gently on the cover of the book.

"What is it?" Tray asked, coming up behind her.

"Silver bookmark," Lilly said.

"That looks promising," Tray said and took it from her, letting the bookmark slide to the floor.

Lilly searched the shelves but found nothing else that related to werewolves or the Aristotle Society.

When they left, they had ten books in hand and the sun was rising.

"I hope reading in the car doesn't make you sick," Patrick said and handed her a book. "We've got plenty of time to kill on the way to Miami."

"Great," Lilly said as she looked down at the book she'd pulled off the shelf.

As they drove away from the Descendants' compound, she started to read. Immediately she was drawn into the story.

Sparah was a witch born of a werewolf father, Gilead, and a witch mother, Fray. Sparah was in love with a vampire king and so she aided in the sealing of Atlantis and it's sinking, allowing herself to go down with the city.

"I think I know why werewolves hate vampires," Lilly mumbled.

"Because they are bloodsucking predators," Dallas said.

Tray grunted and took the book from her, reading over the page quickly. "Sparah, sea witch it says, but apparently half werewolf too. Huh, well I would be pissed if some vamp took my daughter underwater for an eternity too," Tray said.

"She sounds powerful." Lilly took the book back and turned the page. "Do you think they created the Aristotle Society too, to punish the vampires?"

"That doesn't make sense, if Gilead was a werewolf, why would he create tools that would harm him and his kind," Tray pointed out.

"He didn't," Patrick grunted. "Fray and Gilead didn't make it through that night."

"This book was written after oral history twisted and changed the story, but it could still have shades of truth, keep reading," Tray urged.

Lilly read, "Before the sinking the werewolves were born whole, changed at will and although the pull of the moon was strong, they were in control of their bodies."

"Born whole?" Dallas murmured.

"Does that mean their children were born werewolves?" Tray wondered.

"That means something changed after the sinking. Did the Stone go down with Atlantis?"

"The legend of the Stone doesn't speak like it would control all werewolves everywhere, its power is spoken of more like it's usable when needed," Patrick explained.

"But you don't know," Tray said.

Patrick grunted.

Lilly scanned a few more paragraphs. "It doesn't explain, but it does say that the werewolves suffered greatly after the sinking, families were torn apart. The witches were forced to step in and stand between the wolves and the humans." Lilly paused. "Between the wolves and their human family members maybe?"

"It would make sense, if the sudden shift to moon-ruled was too much for many to handle," Tray said.

"That's why they didn't survive the night, Gilead attacked Fray, didn't she," Lilly wondered sadly. "Wouldn't that make witches hate werewolves?"

"Witches created the tools that the Aristotle Society used against us, so that follows," Patrick said. "A way to get back for one of their own being attacked, killed even."

Lilly read some more. "It doesn't mention the Stone or the making of tools, but maybe those came after this was written. Maybe a witch fell in love with a werewolf and created it so they could safely be together," she said a little wistfully. "What if it isn't real," she whispered, and the car was silent as they all mused over that possibility.

"You are only a legend," Tray pointed out. "Yet here you sit; the Blood Moonstone has to be real."

She wanted to believe him. "The witches are refusing to help the Descendants now, or so Julie says. Why do you think that is?"

"That is a very good question," Patrick said. "I've never trusted the witches and whatever motivation they may have to interfere now can't be good for any of us."

"The only thing that motivates is power and revenge," Dallas said.

"And love," Tray added, looking at Lilly.

"We'll stay out of their way if we can," Patrick said.

Lilly closed the book. It was a lot of questions without answers and the more she learned about their sordid history with the vampires and witches, the more she wondered who really were the bad guys. She closed her eyes and leaned her head back. It was a long drive back to Miami, sleep sounded like a good idea.

* * *

Brody watched them drive off and pulled out his phone.

"Yes?" the irritated voice demanded.

"I have an update," Brody said excitedly.

"Well, give it."

"There's a female. A female werewolf," Brody whispered.

"Impossible!"

"I thought so too, but I saw her, I smelled her," he said with glee. "She is with Patrick, Tray, and Dallas. They are headed to Miami. They don't have the Stone, but they took a bunch of books from the Descendants' compound."

"Where has she been? Is she newly turned?"

"The Aristotle Society had her."

"Those bastards are still around?"

"Sounds like they might be down to one last guy in Miami. Name's Brandon and he owns some pawn shop downtown, shouldn't be too hard to find."

"If he was holding a werewolf, then he must still have the collars and rings, a dangerous weapon. You're proving yourself useful, Brody."

"Thank you, sir."

The line went dead, and Brody stared at the entrance to the Descendants' compound and smiled. He was very useful.

A red headed figure snuck through the gate as he watched. She was dressed in all black and moved along close to the wall, obviously trying to remain hidden in the early morning light. He watched her curiously and snuck close enough to realize this was the one that had been with the vampires when they'd captured them. Was she sneaking out at dawn to meet her vampire lover, seemed like bad timing to Brody.

He followed at a safe distance, moving nearly silent on four paws. She stopped in a clearing and looked around expectantly. For a moment Brody thought his cover was blown but her eyes skipped right over the shadow he stood in.

"Sorcha, child," a soft smooth voice slunk through the air as if it tested and tasted everything it touched.

Brody shivered as his ears picked up the words. A green mist stepped out of the shadows across from where he stood watching and coalesced into the form of a woman. She had long black hair and brilliant green eyes. Her skin was the color of caramel and her lips pure black. She was dressed in a long black dress, and she had an emerald green shawl wrapped around her shoulders.

She reminded Brody of a storybook witch, and his instinct was to run, but he couldn't. He was frozen in place and realized that all sounds around him had stopped. There were no birds tweeting, no bugs buzzing, nothing, not even a breeze-rustled leaf made a sound. It was as if the world quit moving in her presence, the earth afraid to breathe.

"I have it," Sorcha said and held up a leather pouch.

"Clever girl, I didn't think you would be able to pry it from your sister's fingers."

"I want it destroyed, that was the deal," Sorcha said.

"Yes, the deal," the witch said, snatching the bag from Sorcha and dumping a bright green stone into her hand. "This is the Descendants' Stone; I will destroy it. And you, child, will get your reward."

The witch reached out and laid one long clawed finger to Sorcha's forehead.

Sorcha screamed, her arms flying out to the side and her back bowed. When she collapsed unmoving the witch laughed and then looked straight at Brody. Her black lips spread in a too wide smile and her eyes seemed to glow.

"Run," she whispered and like a switch the world turned back on. Brody didn't wait around to find out if the girl was alive or not, he took off as fast as he could back to where his car was parked, he hopped in and drove like the devil was on his heels. Maybe she was.

"What the fuck was that?" he hissed after about ten miles stood between him and the Descendants' compound.

He pulled out his phone and stared at it. Should he call someone, should he tell anyone what he'd witnessed?

Forget, ran through his mind and next thing he knew he was sitting on the side of the road slumped over his steering wheel. He woke with a jerk and looked around confused. He rubbed at his head where a sharp pain ran between his eyes.

"What?" he whispered and looked around, the last thing he remembered was watching the redhead leave the compound and then he'd gotten in his truck and now, here he was. "I guess lack of sleep finally caught up with me," he said and started the truck.

Nineteen

TRAY DIDN'T MOVE a muscle as Lilly slept against him. She whined and yipped in her sleep, and he couldn't help smiling as his heart filled. It felt so right to have her against him. He had to figure out a way to make her see it too.

When they got near Miami they turned off and headed toward the cabin where they'd left the collars and ring. If they were lucky, the things would still be sitting there on the ground next to a rotting body.

He doubted they would be that lucky.

Patrick stopped far enough from the trailer that they wouldn't be noticed yet, just in case. Lilly stirred awake beside him, and he bit back a sigh when she moved to sit up. The loss of contact was achingly apparent.

"Are we here?" she asked.

"Back at the trailer," Patrick confirmed, "let's sneak close enough to recon before we decide what to do. If there's nothing on the driveway, we will have to search the trailer and maybe get answers from the sister."

"Brandon's cousin, does that make her an Aristotle too?" Lilly asked.

"I think it was always more of a men's club, I doubt they included her," Patrick said.

"Of course it was, no women Aristotles, no women werewolves," Lilly paused. "Are there women vampires?"

"No," Patrick said.

"What the hell, what do the women get, besides being preyed upon by beasts?"

"Witches and Descendants," Tray pointed out.

They made their way close enough to see that there was no dead body, which meant their hope of an easy recovery of the collars and ring were dashed but it didn't mean they weren't here somewhere.

"I'm going to knock on the door, Dallas come with me. We can sweet talk her, say we were friends with her brother, Glen, right?"

Lilly nodded.

"Okay, you two wait here. I don't see Brandon's van so hopefully she's alone."

Tray watched Patrick and Dallas move forward. He pulled Lilly close, even though they didn't really have to be that careful of being seen, it was a good excuse to hold her tight. She didn't resist and he smiled against her hair, kissing her head softly. She was accepting him more and more and it gave him hope.

"Not the time or place to get frisky," she said with a laugh.

It warmed him to hear her being joyful in a small moment and he gave her a little squeeze. "It's always the right time and place to get frisky, my dear." He wondered if being here was hard for her. This was the last place she'd been a captive. She'd almost died here. For him it was a wonderful place. The first place he'd seen her in human form, held her body and knew that she was free and his.

"Are you okay being here?" he asked.

"Yeah, I want to see this all end."

They watched and listened as Patrick and Dallas approached the trailer door. As long as they kept the conversation outside of the trailer, Tray and Lilly wouldn't have any problem hearing what was said, and they would be able to intervene if something unexpected happened. If the woman did know what they were, and she was equipped to capture them.

It was a longshot, he knew. But that didn't mean he wouldn't be vigilant for danger.

Dallas knocked on the trailer door and they waited, then he knocked again, and a yell came from inside.

"Coming! Keep your damn pants on!"

When the door opened, a woman stood there in a pair of red panties and a see-through white tank top. She had a lit cigarette in her hand and a scowl on her face. It looked like she'd gone to bed with a face full of makeup and was just waking up despite it being late afternoon. Apparently both men were stunned by the sight because no one spoke as she puffed and glared.

"What the hell do you two want?" she finally asked.

"We were friends of your brothers," Patrick said finding his voice.

"Glen's friends?" Her voice softened, obviously she'd cared for her brother. "Funeral is tomorrow." She eyed the two men and smiled. "I can offer you a place to stay for the night," she said, pressing her chest forward.

"We were actually wondering about something he had, some equipment of ours he'd borrowed," Dallas said.

"Equipment?" she said suspiciously and crossed her arms over her chest. "Was he cooking again? Damnit I told him that was not the side of business he had the smarts to be on."

"No, it wasn't drug related. We train dogs. He was trying out some collars we made," Patrick said.

"Those things," she scoffed. "Like I told the other guys, Brandon probably took them when he abandoned me with my dead brother's body," she snapped.

She didn't have the collars, probably not the ring either and that meant Brandon was a valid threat still. Tray couldn't wait to sink his teeth into that man.

Dallas and Patrick took a step away from the door, obviously realizing this was a dead end.

"I'm sorry about your brother," Dallas said sincerely.

"He was a good brother," she said with a sniff and puffed her cigarette. "Funeral is tomorrow if you want to pay your respects. I'd be happy to see you both again. We'll have a proper party after."

They thanked her and walked away, she watched them for a moment then went in and shut the trailer door. Not an ounce of recognition or suspicion on her face. She wasn't Aristotle Society and probably wouldn't believe it if they told her they were werewolves.

"Who else came looking for the collars?" Lilly whispered with fear.

Tray didn't know and that was concerning. He met Patrick's gaze and knew he was thinking the same thing. It could be more Aristotles, and that could be a really big problem.

"Should we call in backup?" Tray asked Patrick as they walked back to the car.

"Not yet, let's find out what we're up against first," Patrick said.

"Let's get the collars before anyone else," Dallas added. "I'll go after the one we took off you, Tray. It's doubtful Brandon went out and found it, that'll be one out of their hands at least."

Patrick nodded and Dallas hurried off in another direction while the rest continued to the car. When he returned with a collar held in a bag to keep it from touching his skin there was a feeling of success, although small, that ran through the group.

"I don't want that anywhere near me," Lilly admitted with a shiver.

"Stick it in the trunk," Patrick agreed.

It was a bit of a somber ride into town, the sun was setting as they pulled in. "Let's check the shop first. If he's not there, I bet we can find his home address easy enough," Patrick said. He glanced at Lilly beside him, she looked nervous, and he wondered if going back to the place where she'd been held captive was going to be too much. She'd handled the trailer fine, but this was different.

He touched her chin, drawing her eyes to his. "Are you okay? You know you don't have to go in if you don't want to. If it's too much. Let us take care of him for you."

"No," she said firmly. "I want to, I want to be part of stopping him for good, stopping all of them."

Her bravery made him proud. She had gained so much strength, both physical and mental in the last few days and he knew it had a lot to do with him, what he'd been able to provide for her and the safety he'd been able to keep her in.

"What's that smell?" Lilly asked as they got to the heart of the city.

They all took deep breaths and let out low growls. "Smells like death," Dallas said.

"I thought Ian captured Norgis and sent him back to Atlantis," Tray snarled.

"I don't think this is Norgis I'm smelling. I caught his scent when we first attacked Ian and the others, this smells different, more... evil? Can evil have a smell?" Patrick asked.

"Yeah, it smells like this," Lilly agreed. "I smelled a monster the first night Brandon took me out, this is different. If Norgis was what I had smelled before, then another monster is in town now."

Tray didn't like any of this. Someone else was after the collars, and there was a monster loose in the city. What had he brought Lilly into and why hadn't the vampires already taken care of this?

* * *

Brandon lounged in his office with his feet up on the desk and spun the ring around his finger. There was a book open in his lap and it wasn't offering him solutions. It spoke of werewolves as abundant and easy to capture. But if that were the case then wouldn't he have heard about it? Someone would have caught the things on a trailcam, and it would be all over the internet. The world was always watching nowadays, things didn't just go around unnoticed.

They were a myth, according to most of the world. Just a fantasy story, but he knew that wasn't true. He knew that there were at least three of the things out there. And although he found it hard to believe that was it, he didn't think there were huge numbers of them either.

So where did they hide and how? More importantly, how was he going to get another one?

Bait, he needed bait and what did werewolves want? Vampires. If he could get a vampire, maybe he could use it to call in a werewolf.

He smiled; the idea had merit.

So how did you call in a vampire to capture?

Blood, human blood. His phone buzzed and distracted him from thoughts of paying homeless men for a pint of the red stuff. Surely, they'd be into it, he had money he could offer.

You had more guys showing up looking for those collars, what the hell are you into? You owe someone money? Rylee had texted.

Brandon smiled; they were coming to him. It would be too easy. Maybe all he had to do was wait for them to come through the door.

"Hey Brandon, you back there?"

He sat up and closed the book quickly. He'd forgotten that Lance was coming in to work tonight.

"Yeah, be right out," Brandon called. He stuffed the collars in a bag along with his gun and a wad of cash then walked out, locking his office behind him.

"Did you hear about the massacre over by the docks? Old warehouse rave, sounds like someone went in and killed like a hundred people," Lance said.

153

"No shit?" Brandon feigned surprise but he knew who it was, the vampires. They were killing people and he was the only one that could stop them. Too bad his weapon had run off with her boyfriend. He gripped his bag tighter, he needed one so he could do his job, make his daddy proud.

"Oh yeah, police are all over the city searching and warning people to keep an eye out for anything suspicious."

"Well, be careful tonight, I'm out." Brandon walked out the door full of determination. This was his city, and he was going to protect it. He'd leash a werewolf or two then they'd go hunting. "Watch out vamp bastards," he called out, causing a few people to look at him funny. "Brandon's coming for your asses," he added as a couple decided to cross to the other side of the street in front of him.

All those stupid citizens had no idea what was out there, what he stood in front of. Maybe he'd bring one in and record it burning in the sunlight, show them what they needed to fear and why they needed to show him some fucking respect.

The Aristotle Society was the savior of the people, chosen to be the line of defense between man and beast.

He was a fucking superhero.

Twenty

LILLY WAS nervous as they parked close to the pawn shop. She didn't know if walking in there was going to trigger her fight or flight, so she stayed close to Tray, soaking in his calm. The smell of him reminded her she wasn't alone and that went a long way to settling her nerves.

The city was lit up by streetlights and there was plenty of noise, cars, and people, but there was something more. There was something heavy in the air. Not just the stench of what was apparently a monster from the deep, but also death, blood, and death. It wasn't what the city normally smelled of, not what she'd scented when she'd been out with Brandon not that long ago and it twisted in her gut. It made her want to shift and run and save. She wanted to protect the innocent from whatever was going on.

"You don't have to go in," he whispered again, sensing her rising stress.

"Yes, I do. If I don't face what he did to me, I'll never be able to let it go." And she did want to let it go. Spending the last couple days with Tray and his packmates had started to fill in a hole that was so deep it had been consuming her. But little by little she was starting to realize that belonging to their pack, maybe even belonging to Tray, wasn't what she was afraid of. Being a part of a pack wasn't being owned. Patrick didn't want to control, she could see that in his interactions with his packmates and with his wife. It was safety, it was home, and it was comfort.

Of course she wasn't ready to tell Tray all that. He was possessive enough already, if she told him she might like it, she was certain he'd overwhelm her.

"Why don't you two wait outside while we go in and check things out?" Patrick was saying as they rounded a corner.

"No, I want to go in and confront him," Lilly said firmly, her steps solid and her back straight. She was pulling on every ounce of determination and courage she had, but she was going to see this through.

When they got close to the shop, they all froze and stared for a moment. The door was busted off its hinges and inside the place was tossed like someone had picked up the entire building and shook the whole damn thing. The scent of fresh blood was coming from inside and Lilly froze. Was this it? Was Brandon dead in there? She was surprised at how disappointing that thought was, that she would have missed the opportunity to kill him, to tell him that she was going to live forever, free and happy and his insignificant human light was being snuffed out by the weapon he thought he was special enough to control.

"I will be disappointed if Brandon is already dead," Tray growled, reading her mind.

"Me too," Lilly agreed.

"Do you smell that?" Dallas said carefully and they all breathed deep.

"Werewolves," Patrick growled. "Not mine."

"The men who were asking about the collars," Dallas said and sniffed again. "It must be Weston's pack, but how the hell did they know? And how did they get so deep into our territory without being noticed?"

"Good question," Patrick said darkly and started forward.

They followed, Tray had a tight grip on Lilly's arm but she didn't complain, she was terrified of meeting Weston and his pack. She'd call Tray her mate and promise to have his adorable little babies if some other alpha thought to make her his.

"I've got you," Tray whispered, sensing her distress.

There were sirens in the distance, but they didn't sound like they were getting closer, maybe no one had called in this crime scene yet.

They stepped over broken glass and splintered wood into the shop.

Everything was on the floor. It looked like the wolves had been trying to destroy everything in sight.

"Find the body," Patrick said, and they spread out.

Tray led Lilly along one side of the room toward the counter. Behind it were two doors, one led to the basement and the other probably an office. As they got close, she couldn't keep her eyes off the door that led to that horrible place downstairs. She started to breathe heavily, her mind spiraling toward panic and she felt her muscles ripple, wanting to shift to wolf and run as far and as fast as possible.

"Lilly," Tray said and pulled her into a hug. "Lilly, let's wait outside," he insisted.

"No," she said firmly, she needed to see this through. She needed to be here and be free, she needed to walk in and out of this place on two feet of her own free will. She pushed away from him and went forward until she stood in front of the basement door. Her hand reached out to touch the knob.

"Found it!" Dallas shouted making her jump and turn. He was lifting up a display case that had been pushed over and looking down at a mangled body. Bitten and bloody, there was no doubt this was a werewolf kill. "Not Brandon," he said.

"Good," Tray said darkly.

Lilly let out a relieved breath.

"Office is destroyed, if there was anything useful in there, it's gone. We need to find this guy before Weston's pack does," Patrick said coming out of the office.

"We need to warn the pack that we've been invaded," Dallas said, dropping the display back down onto the body.

"No," Patrick said.

"We can't let Weston get away with this," Tray scoffed.

"We won't, but think about it. How did he know? Someone in our pack is working for him. I bet when his guys showed up last time they recruited a little help before they were killed and someone's been feeding Weston information since."

"Shit," Tray hissed.

"Yeah, so for now, it's just us," Patrick said.

"Then let's hunt," Dallas said excitedly.

"We need to go after Brandon," Patrick said. "He's the target and we can intercept Weston's pack at the same time."

"What about the monster?" Lilly pointed out. "There's something out there terrorizing the city too."

Patrick sighed heavily. "I think we have to trust the vamps to clean up their mess, the monster is theirs unless we run across it. We need to stop Brandon, and the intruding wolves. That's our responsibility."

Lilly wasn't completely comfortable with the idea of trusting the vampires to take care of things without excess bloodshed, but she also didn't want to argue with an alpha, so she just nodded. As they walked back across the shop, she glanced over her shoulder to the door she hadn't opened.

It was enough to know she could have. She wasn't being forced in or out of this place and she was on two feet. That was healing and the hole in her soul filled in a little bit more.

"How are we going to find Brandon?" Tray asked as they walked away from the shop.

Lilly had a terrifying thought. She froze, and the men stopped after a couple steps, turning to look back at her questioningly.

"What is it, Lilly?"

"Brandon is going to go after the vampires," she said with a gasp.

"What?" Patrick asked.

"Think about it. He wants werewolves, he's pissed, and he has at least two collars to strap down werewolves with. But he doesn't know how to catch one, except maybe to tempt it in. He's a hunter, a trapper. I've heard him and Glen talk about it with gators. They bait a trap and wait and watch then bam, got the sucker."

"So what does that have to do with the vampires?" Tray asked.

"He's dumb enough to think he can trap a vamp then use it to trap a wolf," she said.

"Shit," Patrick said.

"Yeah," Lilly said.

"The question is, where do we try and head him off?" Tray said. "While he's trying to catch a vampire or wait and see if he survives that and while he's trying to catch a werewolf?"

"He'll never survive against a vamp and I want the satisfaction of a werewolf making the kill. I think we have to split up and criss-cross the city," Patrick said. "Tray, you take Lilly and start at the beach, work your way west. Dallas and I will start here and work our way south."

Lilly gripped Tray's arm, it made her nervous to split up from the others, but she didn't want to seem like a weak link, so she didn't say anything.

They all shifted to wolf to heighten their senses. Patrick and Dallas set out, moving north and south. Lilly and Tray ran to the beach then headed west one street at a time. What they encountered was horrifying. The humans who were still on the streets were frantic, their conversations all centered around the murders. Massacred bodies were being discovered all over the city with no particular pattern or reason and it wasn't long before Lilly and Tray didn't encounter any humans at all aside from the cops and emergency personnel who were working to save the wounded and hunt the killer.

She barely caught a hint of vampire on the air and that was concerning. Why weren't the vamps out here stopping this? But more concerning was the scent of unknown werewolf they encountered more than once.

She felt her strength start to wane after a few hours. She still wasn't back to full health, and she knew she was going to start holding Tray back soon. But he didn't complain, just matched her speed and stride, and stayed close. He wasn't going to leave her behind unprotected. She gave him an appreciative yip and licked playfully at his face as they sped across a small park.

He growled playfully back and bumped against her side.

The distraction was short, but it was enough for the other wolf to get a drop on them.

A large grey wolf appeared from behind a bush and tackled Tray. Tray immediately was up and fighting back. The two were rolling and biting at each other, then falling apart and circling. The grey wolf was just as big as Tray and clearly knew how to fight too.

Lilly panicked; she didn't know what to do. She knew she couldn't really help Tray, so she just watched and whined as they crashed together again, teeth bared and claws slashing. She smelled blood and had no idea whose it was. Her heart broke as she imagined Tray dying, imagined this other wolf claiming her as his prize from battle.

She couldn't let that happen, so she ran.

She ran blindly as the hole in her soul widened. She was alone, she wouldn't be safe unless she got far away. She ran and ran until she hit a rock awkwardly with one foot and fell, skidding across an alleyway and landing with a crash against a dumpster.

Scared and hurt, she scrambled up and around to hide behind the dumpster and lick her wound. A rat screeched at her and skittered away; she was alone.

She didn't know what to do, wasn't sure where she was or how far from Tray she'd gotten, but she was certain he was dead, he was dead and she would never be able to tell him that maybe she did want to have his adorable little babies and maybe she did want to be a part of Patrick's pack and be best friends with Mary. She wanted to meet the other wives and watch children grow up and play and choose to become a werewolf or not.

She wanted all of that, and now she couldn't have it.

A growl sounded at the end of the alley and she backed up, biting back a whine as she stepped on her hurt paw, she knew it wasn't broken but it still hurt like hell. She must have twisted the ankle. She tried to scent who was in the alley, but the acrid smell of garbage overwhelmed her senses.

Paws padded closer and another low growl sounded, then a howl, whoever it was had scented her.

Fuck.

Her breaths came in pants, her eyes started to blacken as her body threatened to panic and pass out. This wasn't happening, she wasn't being hunted, no way.

"What did you find?" A familiar voice said, filling her with terror and she went full into flight mode.

Despite her hurt paw, she launched herself to the top of the dumpster and just as she was about to leap off it and down the alley, she heard the shot, felt the sting of impact, and then she was falling to the ground.

She blinked up at the familiar face, but she didn't even have the ability to growl. Brandon had tranquilized her. An unfamiliar white wolf sniffed her and howled again.

"Oh yes, she's a girl and you two are going to make me some pups," Brandon said, just as the darkness fully took her. "What's the matter, you weren't into redheads?" he sneered at her.

Twenty-One

BRANDON COULDN'T BELIEVE his luck! First, he'd found this white wolf sniffing around the alley where he'd found that first vamp a few days ago. It had been so distracted by some scent up the building's fire escape that Brandon had been able to sneak close and whip a silver chain around him quick enough to subdue the beast. Then the collar had gone on and that was it. All his.

Now this, the little bitch who'd dared to escape him was back. He put the collar on her with a little trouble due to his injured hand, but he managed to get it on tight as the white wolf looked on.

"I hope you like her, she's trouble, but I want pups," he told the white wolf who just tilted his head and then howled again. "What the hell do you keep doing that for?" Brandon snapped and yanked on the male's leash. "If animal control shows up, I'm going to be pissed. Do you want to be neutered?"

"He's calling in his alpha," a smooth deep voice said from the end of the alley.

Brandon jumped and turned. A man stood there dressed in all black. The light was behind him, and Brandon couldn't make out any facial features and it made for a very intimidating picture, not that he'd ever admit to fearing anyone, or anything.

He stiffened and raised his gun at the intruder. "Alpha, huh, not anymore, I'm in charge of these animals now. Well, I don't have a collar for you, so I'll just have to kill you," Brandon said. His hand shook slightly, but his voice was strong and he was confident with the beast on a leash beside him and the bitch passed out at his feet. He was the top of this food chain.

"You won't kill me," the man said confidently and took a step forward into a slice of moonlight. He had short brown hair and bright blue eyes that never wavered from Brandon's face. He walked with surety until he was only a few steps away from the end of Brandon's gun.

"You obviously don't know me," Brandon said, but his voice had lost some confidence. There was something very strange about this man, something that made Brandon's skin crawl.

"I know your kind, the Aristotle Society. You all thought you were so much better than us just because you had a witch to help you along the way. But look who's survived. You're the last one I hear, and the werewolves are plenty. The witches bet on the wrong team."

"I will recruit more," Brandon said and the wolf beside him growled. "Stay back or I'll tell him to attack."

"He won't, I'm his alpha and you put the wrong collar on him," the man said with a grin that transformed into a snout snarling. It was only the second time Brandon had seen a transition and the one at the museum had been fast and full, this was something else. Only the man's face changed and transitioned seamlessly into his neck making him look like something from a horror movie.

Brandon was petrified.

The alpha wolf leaped forward and gripped Brandon by the throat just as the white wolf lurched forward and chomped down on his arm, forcing him to drop the gun as a shot went off. The bullet slammed harmlessly into a nearby building's wall.

Brandon hit the ground knowing it was over, he couldn't breathe, couldn't scream and his bowels had already released. The last thing he saw before he died was the face of death, a vengeful angel of fire. She touched his head, burning him from the inside out as the last of his life was twisted.

"Death is too good for you," Death whispered, and her hood fell back to reveal the face of a white wolf. So eerily similar to what the alpha had looked like before attacking.

Brandon would have screamed if his vocal cords hadn't been severed.

* * *

Weston stepped back from the body. Matt sat so he could take the collar off, his second in command. Then he knelt down next to the beautiful black female and gasped. "Is this one connected to the ring?" Weston asked.

Matt shifted to human and rubbed at his neck. "Might be. He has a couple collars with him but just one ring. He didn't mention the Stone, but if he has all of this, I bet it's in his apartment. Dumbass might not even realize what it is. He bragged about how he has a whole stash of the collars at home too. Leftover from when they had a whole pack of werewolves to command. He seemed to think he was headed in the direction of having that again," Matt said with a laugh. "Idiot doesn't seem to realize how the rings work."

"Yeah, we didn't find it at the shop. Grab his wallet for an address and I'll call the guys to come grab her before the tranquilizer wears off. Get that collar off of her, I don't want her freaking out when she wakes up," Weston ordered.

"Sure thing, boss make sure his ring is off first."

Weston grunted and grabbed the ring off the dying man's

finger then pulled out his phone and fired off the necessary texts. He slipped both back in his pocket and his eyes darted around. He'd been playing hide and seek with that damn monster all night and now he knew that Patrick was in town with a couple of his wolves. If they got to the Stone before him, then their play for control of the U.S. would be lost.

He looked down at the female and grinned. Of course they did have quite the bargaining chip now.

"Got it," Matt said, standing up with the wallet. "But are you sure we can just leave her here?"

"Yeah, the Stone is more important, and my car is too far away. Reggie and Harold should be on their way for her, no time to waste."

Matt shifted back to wolf and Weston took off, entering the address on Brandon's driver's license into his phone's GPS. He was so close to his goal now he could taste it.

As they rounded the corner of the alley there was a terrible scream followed by the sound of cracking bones behind them.

"What the hell?" Weston hissed, but he didn't go back. If the monster had found the bodies and decided to have a snack, that was fine, he had more important things to work toward.

Twenty-Two

TRAY HEARD and felt the satisfying snap of the grey wolf's neck in his jaws. He was bloody and pretty sure a rib was cracked, but he'd won in the end.

He lifted his head expecting to see a proud Lilly waiting to congratulate him on the kill.

She was gone.

He howled mournfully then took off after her scent as images of the most horrifying scenarios filled his mind.

He followed as fast as he could, but she had run in no predictable manner, and he lost her trail a couple times when it was muddied with the scent of another werewolf or the monster that was still stalking through the city. His frustration rose with every step that didn't take him to her, and fear like nothing he'd ever known filled him. What if he didn't find her in time? He didn't even want to consider the eternal stretch of life without her. He would rather her choose to leave him, he could stalk her for eternity, watch her from a distance. But if she were dead, he wouldn't want to continue living either.

He neared an alley and froze. He approached slowly, afraid of what he was about to see. He could tell there was blood, he could smell unfamiliar wolf and Lilly. But when he turned the corner to the dark stretch, he didn't see her. He approached the writhing shadow that lay on the ground hoping for answers.

A twisted form lay naked and bloody. The wounds looked life ending but for some reason that Tray couldn't fathom, the great goddess of death had chosen him to live, to shift and change and walk on the earth as a child of the moon.

Tray was tempted to take Brandon's life as he stared down at him suffering through his first change. It would be merciful to end his suffering in those moments. No matter how far from his own changing Tray got, he would never forget the pain he had endured. It took the strongest to survive it and the blessing of Her.

Brandon deserved the pain, but he didn't deserve the honor of surviving it.

Tray shifted to human and stood naked over the trembling man. Brandon's lower half was fully formed into a wolf now.

"You don't deserve this honor. But you do deserve the pain and when I find Lilly, I will let her tear your throat out."

Tray shifted back to wolf and sniffed around until he once again had her scent, then he hurried off. It was much harder this time, so mixed with another werewolf. It nearly made him blind with rage to know that she was likely harmed and being carried by another werewolf, someone in Weston's pack. What horrors waited for her in the pack that had bred the men who had attacked Sorcha?

Head down on the scent, he nearly ran into Dallas and Patrick as their paths crossed. Tray snapped and snarled before he realized who it was, then he shifted to human.

Patrick shifted as well.

"Where's Lilly?" Patrick demanded.

"I was attacked by one of Weston's wolves and she ran off terrified while I was distracted. By the time I tracked her scent to an alley I found Brandon," Tray took a steadying breath. "He's changing and she's gone. Weston has her."

"Shit."

"Yeah, I'm tracking her scent now."

"We'll follow," Patrick said and shifted back to wolf.

Tray shifted as well, and they took off following the scent. It ended in a parking lot and Tray howled mournfully to the sky, letting all of his anguish out. Tracking her now would be nearly impossible.

Dallas and Patrick joined his cry, filling the night with their sorrow.

Patrick shifted first and the others followed suit.

"What do we do now?" Dallas asked.

"We can't leave Brandon, he's too dangerous until he learns to control himself," Patrick pointed out.

Dallas got a wicked grin on his face. "Let me take care of that, I know where there's a nice little cell for him to be safe in until we can decide what's to be done with him."

Patrick nodded and Dallas shifted again and took off.

"I'm going after her," Tray snarled before Patrick could order him to do anything different.

"I know you are," Patrick said. "I need to make sure the city is secure. I won't leave if any of Weston's men are still here and as soon as Brandon can talk, I'm finding out if he has the Stone."

"I'll contact you when I find her."

They hugged briefly and Tray shifted, following the very faint scent of her down the road. He would find her because he couldn't accept any other option.

* * *

Lilly woke slowly, head groggy and her limbs were heavy. "Tray?" she whispered.

"No," a voice said cheerfully. "I am Weston, your new alpha."

Lilly sat up and her head spun, she didn't let herself fall back down though and she clutched what covering she had to her naked body as she looked around. She was in a small room, two beds, bad carpet, and a desk. It smelled like cigarettes, and she could hear the sound of passing cars outside.

"Where are we?"

"Motel, on our way west, back to my territory. Though, soon it will all be mine," he said darkly and held up a large red stone.

"The Blood Moonstone," she gasped. It had to be, she could feel the pulse of power it gave off and it tickled her skin.

"Yep, that little twerp Brandon had it in his apartment. Probably didn't have any idea what it was, just something passed down with you and the collars." He looked at her and his lips twisted into a wicked grin. His young face took on the look that one gets through years of debauchery, and it terrified her. "We smelled you in the shop, my men went insane when they scented a female werewolf. They destroyed the place and ripped the guy apart before I could even question him." Weston shrugged. "I should have warned them there was a rumor of you, but I wasn't sure I believed it myself."

The life of a nobody human meant nothing to him, and Lilly felt fear crawl up her spine. This man wasn't a werewolf who wanted to protect humans, this was a man who wanted to use his wolf to take and overpower. A true monster.

"Do you think this will allow you to carry a child?" He asked with a raised eyebrow as he rolled the Stone around in his hand.

Lilly couldn't answer, her throat was closed, and she tried to shift but couldn't. Why couldn't she change? She needed to jump out the nearest window and run.

"Oh, not sure if you knew this but, the Stone will keep you locked into whatever form you're in, human is what I prefer for mating."

"Fuck you," she managed.

"That's the plan," he said with a laugh.

"I'm pregnant," she said as he set the Stone down on the table behind him.

"Pregnant?" he growled.

She nodded emphatically. "Tray and I have mated multiple times. I am pregnant and it won't abort until after the full moon change." She was almost certain she wasn't pregnant and if she *had* gotten pregnant by Tray, she was pretty sure the first time she'd shifted to wolf it would have aborted. But she needed to say something to delay Weston. Tray would come for her; she knew he would. If he was alive.

She pushed that thought from her mind, it was too painful.

"The full moon is next week. I can wait that long, I suppose."

"If you come near me, I'll bite off any appendage I can reach," she promised. "No matter what form I'm in."

He just laughed. "You're lucky I like my women with a bit of fire." He walked to the door, Stone in hand. "Don't even think about trying anything. You can't shift and I won't be that far away. I've got two men outside on guard duty too. You've got a week to like the idea of breeding my pups, or you won't get to rule by my side, you'll just be my bitch in bed. If you were able to handle the turn, I can find another female who can, too."

"Rule what?" she couldn't help asking.

"Everything! We are the dominant species on land. The vampires are too afraid to come out of hiding farther than the coasts because they know it and nothing on land is more powerful than us. We never should have been subjugated by humans," he spat. "The witches have paid for that little stunt and the Descendants pose no threat now either." He smiled a sickening smile. "I'm a very old wolf, love. And I am ready to rule all that was promised to me."

He walked out and she wanted to throw something at the door but there wasn't anything not bolted down other than the pillow and that wouldn't give a satisfying smash. So she settled for screaming. The responding laughter she heard outside broke her. She crumpled and cried because she didn't know what else to do.

When the tears dried up she took a deep breath then took

stock of the situation. She felt her ankle, it was swollen and sore, but not broken. There was a bruise on her side where Brandon had shot her with a tranquilizer dart, but other than that she was fine. Aside from not being able to shift to wolf.

She wrapped the sheet tight around her body and hobbled to the bathroom, she locked herself inside.

"Tray, I'm sorry I ran off, please don't be dead, please save me," she whispered, knowing that she was likely going to have to save herself. She leaned her head against the wall and thought about everything she knew. Weston was from the west coast, he was the only other alpha in the States, and he was, apparently, old. He had a grudge and was on a major power trip so she supposed that fit with him being old. She remembered her father talking about old alphas and how they ran their packs different than him, more wild, more savage. He'd warned her not to leave his territory and she hadn't, at least not voluntarily. She was going to have to be careful, she likely couldn't physically stop him, but maybe she could outsmart him. She already had bought herself some time with her pregnancy lie, so he wasn't infallible. She had hope and she clung to that thought, fashioning the thin sheet into a sort of toga and leaving the bathroom in search of a weapon.

A half hour later she had discerned that there wasn't a single usable weapon in the room, nor was there a stitch of clothing. The sun was up, and the clock said it was almost noon. She'd been out for nearly twelve hours. How long they'd driven before stopping, she had no idea. There was no phone, not that she would know who to call anyway and if she were honest, she had no idea how to work the thing that barely resembled what she'd used a few times a hundred years ago.

She sat on the bed, frustrated, and stared at the wall, plotting how she would dig her teeth and nails into Weston if he touched her. Human or not, she would tear him to pieces. She had no interest in being a part of his power play.

When the door opened and Weston walked in with a bag

smelling of greasy food, she wanted to yell at him but her stomach rumbled and she decided to wait and see what he would do next.

"Food, and some clothing since we won't be rolling in the sack just yet. We'll stay the night here; I have an injured man next door and there's a local doctor that is going to stitch him up."

"Aw, did Tray hurt your poor puppy?" she sneered.

"Tray killed Carter," Weston said with a tight frown.

Lilly's insides lit up. He was alive, he'd gotten away from the grey wolf that had attacked him. He would come for her; she was certain of it. She couldn't hold back her smile as she accepted the bag of food and pulled out a burger. She tore it open and started to eat.

"So what happened to the other one?" she asked around a mouthful of meat and bun.

"Had a run-in with some kind of monster. Fucking thing was vicious. I don't know what made him stop from killing Simon. I came up to them fighting and the thing threw Simon, walked two steps to grab at him again then jerked as if he'd come up to a wall, then snarled, shrunk down to the size of a man, and walked away. It was the craziest thing I've ever seen."

Lilly didn't even try to make sense of the story Weston gave her; it wasn't what mattered anyway. "If Tray is alive, he'll come for me."

"He won't win against us," Weston assured her and stood. "I'll be back in a few hours with dinner. If you get bored, I think this place has free porn." He motioned to the black box on the dresser. "Do you know how this works? How long since you were human? When did the Aristotle Society capture you?"

Lilly just looked at him blankly. He didn't deserve to know her.

He shrugged and left. When he shut the door behind him, she took the bag of clothes to the bathroom and dressed, happy to have more than a sheet covering her. It was a rather short skirt though and a tight shirt, so she didn't feel a ton better and of course he hadn't bothered with underwear.

"What is with men and not thinking about underwear," she grumbled as she tugged on the skirt to make sure it was covering her ass before she stepped back out into the motel room.

She heard a scream through the wall and pressed an ear to it.

"What the hell?" She heard Weston snap in the other room.

"I have to rebreak it so it heals straight," a feminine voice snapped back. "You should have stopped sooner and set it right."

"We didn't have time. We had to get away from the city," Weston said.

"Yeah, I hear they're still finding bodies," the feminine voice said.

Well, she knew where the injured wolf was. Lilly went back to the bed and sat down, staring at the covered window. It looked like the sun was starting to set, the light becoming a warmer tone. "Tray, where are you?" she whispered.

Twenty-Three

TRAY SAT in shadow across from a cheap motel along the highway. He'd tracked them here and he was exhausted. He never stopped running once he was on her trail and his body wanted to give up. It didn't take long for him to figure the situation. Lilly was in the room being guarded by two werewolves. In the room next to that was an injured werewolf and Weston had been in and out of both rooms. They took a human into the one with the injured werewolf. She must be some kind of doctor judging by the bag she had carried with her.

They weren't moving any time soon he decided, so he took the opportunity to slip away and hunt a few rabbits and find water. He needed the strength; he couldn't risk losing her because he'd neglected simply eating. Then he did something he wasn't proud of; he broke into a nearby house and stole a phone.

He had to contact the others.

"Hello," Patrick said cautiously, not recognizing the number.

"Hey, they've stopped."

"Where?"

"Outside of Tallahassee."

"I'm on the way, probably a couple hours out though. We

didn't find anything at Brandon's apartment, it was completely turned over though, so if he had anything, I'm sure Weston got it first."

"Where is Brandon now?"

"Locked up in his cell waiting for Lilly to decide his fate. Dallas is babysitting."

"I'm going in after her as soon as I can. I won't wait for you."

"I figured, though I wish you wouldn't go alone. I could send someone your way at least maybe, I'll put out a call and see who is near there."

"Okay, but make sure whoever it is knows that she's the top priority, next is the Stone and the collars."

"Will do. Be safe brother."

Tray hung up and slunk back to the shadow across the highway where he could watch and plot. He figured when the sun was fully down he could sneak up on her room from the back. Maybe he could bust down the wall and grab her. It didn't look like a well-made building.

As he watched, Weston came out of the injured werewolf's room with the human woman. They were arguing and he slapped her, hard. She stumbled back and he grabbed her wrist, pulling her to him then continued to spit words at her too quiet for Tray to hear.

The way he treated women was no surprise and Tray wanted to kill him right then. How dare he think he deserved the honor of being a werewolf, let alone an alpha. He'd forgotten that their mission was protection, not dominance.

Tray couldn't wait to remind him.

The woman pushed him away and slapped him back, then got in her car as fast as she could and sped away. Weston adjusted his crotch and walked back into the injured wolf's room.

An hour later Tray scented a packmate and a black and white wolf laid down in the shadow next to him then shifted. "What's up, lady trouble?"

"You were in the area, Brody?" Tray asked in surprise. Brody lived much farther north and had recently been at least ten hours in the other direction watching over the Descendants.

"I like to roam. Lucky for you."

"Great, it's almost dark enough we can risk getting closer and make a grab for her. She's in room twelve there and eleven is where they have an injured werewolf. It's Weston and two others, healthy and guarding her."

Brody nodded. "Cool, cool, okay so we run in and grab, run off. Seems like a solid plan."

Tray eyed him curiously, he seemed nervous, his pulse was high, and he wasn't meeting Tray's eye.

"Hey look, Weston's leaving, now's probably the time to go in," Brody said.

Tray looked back and sure enough, Weston was heading out in a car, no doubt to get food. They probably wouldn't have a better opportunity. One of the guards was still in front of Lilly's door but the other was in with the injured packmate.

"I'll distract, you run in," Brody said and shifted, then bolted across the street before Tray could argue that it wasn't a great plan.

"Damnit," Tray growled and shifted, then raced across the street.

The guard outside Lilly's door had taken off after Brody and they were around the building already, leaving Tray a clear path to her. He tried to shift back to human and couldn't. *What the fuck?* He growled. It had to be the Stone. Weston had found the thing, it both thrilled and frustrated him. He scratched furiously at the door and yipped for Lilly's attention.

"What the hell?" Lilly opened the door at the same time the door to the injured wolf opened.

The other guard pulled a gun and shot Tray twice without hesitation. He went down hard and fast.

"Tray!" Lilly screamed and threw herself on top of him.

Tray breathed in her scent as darkness washed away the pain.

176

* * *

Lilly screamed, "Stop! Stop, I'll do anything, just stop!"

There wasn't another shot but she still didn't move, covering Tray with her body, she sobbed. She felt him move under her, he was still breathing, she couldn't let them shoot him again.

A hand touched her shoulder and she stiffened. "Please, just don't kill him."

"No worries, darling, help me move his body inside."

Lilly startled and looked up, seeing a familiar face. This wasn't one of Weston's men, this was the wolf who Patrick had talked to outside of the Descendants' compound, Brody.

"What's going on?" she whispered, eyes darting around. Was this her rescue, had he already killed the others?

"Had to cross the damn street to get far enough from the Stone to shift back to human," he grunted. "That's a little annoying."

Lilly was confused, she scooted out of the way as the man scooped up Tray's body with some effort and carried him into the room and dumped him on the bed.

"My name's Brody."

"I know. You're Patrick's wolf," she said quietly, feeling dumb.

"Was, but Weston offered me a better position. I don't want to be the low man on the totem. I want to eat the sweet meat, fresh, next to the alpha." He walked to the bathroom and she heard the water running as he washed his hands clean of Tray's blood.

"You turned on your alpha," Lilly gasped. She was standing near the open door and as far as she could tell there was no guard outside. Could she run fast enough to get away? Could she leave Tray here wounded?

She knew she couldn't, and she hurried to his side, looking for the wounds. She found one on his chest, it went straight out the other side and already showed signs of healing but by his shaky breathing, she guessed that the bullet had nicked a lung. There was nothing she could do for it but hope his healing would be swift enough. She looked for the other one and found it near his right upper arm, straight into his chest, probably near his heart. She pressed her ear to him and reassured herself that it was beating steadily.

"Forgive me," she whispered and dug her fingers deep into the hole, fishing around for the bullet.

He whined and twitched.

"What the hell are you doing? We can call the nurse back," Brody said, coming out of the bathroom.

"Fuck you," she snapped.

He just chuckled and sat on the bed, watching her struggle.

It took way longer than she was comfortable with, but with his body working to expel the bullet and her digging deep despite the gag reflex, she got the bullet and pulled it out, looking at it with a frown.

"Silver tipped wood," she gasped.

"Works for all evil," Brody said.

"Get me a towel," she demanded.

He did and she pressed it to the wound with all her strength. Lilly closed her eyes and prayed to the goddess of death that she spare this man, this wolf. He was far too good to die like this, without her being able to tell him that she did want all the things with him. The home, the family, the life. She wanted him to take care of her, to be her everything and she didn't care that she didn't even have a legal name to herself. She wanted to be his and she wanted him to be hers and she wanted Patrick's pack, the friends and family. It was every werewolf's dream, at least she'd always assumed it was.

"How could you betray your pack?" she asked Brody.

"Here," he said, handing her a belt.

She took it and with great effort she managed to tie it around Tray and over the towel firmly. She could tell the bleeding was already slowing. Without the silver in him, he would heal quickly.

Thankfully he hadn't been hit with a tranquilizer dart, they couldn't afford that kind of wait time.

"Why?" she asked again, sitting next to Tray on the bed and looking at Brody. "How?"

"I didn't grow up in Patrick's pack. Kind of like Tray, and you. I was part of a pack that was wiped out by the virus. I was on track to be alpha, my father was alpha, his father before him too. But when I joined with Patrick I had to start at the bottom. I won't accept less than I deserve, less than I was born for."

"Why didn't you just explain to Patrick that you wanted to move up?"

"Don't you think I tried? But he had his favorite, Dallas, and then when he showed up," Brody glared at Tray, "that was that. No room for advancement unless I wanted to make my own pack, which I was tempted to do, but then this opportunity came my way from Weston."

"And you think being higher up in Weston's pack is better than waiting to move up in Patrick's? Weston is a psycho."

"You don't know who Weston is, do you?" Brody sneered. "I'm not surprised, I don't think Patrick knows either and that is going to be a very big mistake."

Lilly's stomach sank. "Who is he?"

Brody leaned forward and smiled wide, baring his teeth at her. "He is the son of Gilead, and he wants revenge for the death of his father."

Gilead. That name pinged in her mind. Fray's husband and father of the witch who fell in love with the vampire king.

"Gilead was killed because he became feral, uncontrollable after the sinking." Lilly was just guessing.

"Yes, he took his wife's life in anger as the moon started to rule us. The witches killed him in revolt for their queen's death. Weston survived in shadow for a long time, waiting for the opportunity to come to power."

"Why now?"

"It's not for us to know, we just get to take advantage of the benefits. He removed all the witches west of the Mississippi and most of the Descendants. No one can stand against us, no one is more powerful than the werewolves."

"You could still let us go. You have the Stone." She gave him a hopeful look.

"Let the only female werewolf in existence go? He'd skin me alive and make me into a rug. No, you are not going anywhere." He glanced at Tray. "You saved his life just now but for what? When Weston returns with dinner, he's probably just going to order him dead and then we're out of here. Simon isn't healed yet, but Patrick is on his way so we can't hang out any longer." Brody got up and walked to the door. "Don't do anything stupid, I'd hate to hurt you. Keep in mind that there's a lot Weston could do to you and you'd still be alive and able to breed."

"I know," she whispered as the door shut. Tears fell and she laid her body over Tray, weeping and shivering. What were they going to do?

Twenty-Four

BRANDON WOKE UP WITH A START, the memory of pain beyond anything he ever wanted to endure rushed through him and he opened his mouth to scream.

A howl came out.

He jumped and turned, eyes searching for the beast. All he saw were bars and a pile of blankets. He heard the slide of chains. He saw a flash of brown fur and turned to catch it, but it turned too. He reached out a hand to grab it.

He saw a paw with big claws, and he jumped back. He fell in a twisted heap, tail in his face, his eyes nearly crossed, and he saw a long snout with a big black nose.

He was a werewolf.

He howled again and jumped to his feet and looked around again. He realized he was in the basement of the shop, in her cage, wearing her chains.

He collapsed in a panting heap and whined. This was a fate worse than death.

"Did I hear you making noise down there?" a voice called from the top of the stairs. Footsteps followed and soon a large man was standing in front of the cage.

Brandon recognized him from when they'd first taken the other male wolf. He'd shot this guy, but he was fine by the looks of it. He was a werewolf too, certainly he wouldn't leave Brandon in here to die. He probably just had to keep him in here for safety of first waking up. Surely he would let Brandon out soon, let him turn human again.

"My name is Dallas and I'm your babysitter until Lilly decides what your punishment should be," he said calmly and walked over to the freezer. He pulled out a frozen steak and walked to the bars. "Is this the shit she was expected to survive on? No wonder she was half dead," he said angrily. Dallas squatted down and looked through the bars straight into Brandon's eyes.

Brandon backed up and cowered, he couldn't help himself. His instincts were telling him this was someone he had to listen to.

"You don't deserve anything better. I hope those chains burn your skin and the hunger for fresh meat claws at your stomach." Dallas tossed the steak into the cage and turned, walked back up the stairs and through the door.

Brandon heard the door locks click and his stomach twisted with fear.

He stared down at the steak, his stomach grumbled even as his mind rejected the idea of eating raw frozen meat. He walked over and sniffed it, it didn't smell great, but it smelled good enough. He ate it up in two bites and his stomach grumbled for more.

He walked over to the pile of dirty blankets and laid down. They smelled like her, a pleasant scent he had to admit. He'd always thought she smelled awful, like dog only wilder, but now her scent was tantalizing. Lilly, her name was Lilly. It felt weird to know that. He looked at the bars and whined.

Something told him he was never getting out.

* * *

Lilly knew she had to do something. It had been twenty minutes and Tray was still passed out. Weston would no doubt be back any minute and then it would be over. He'd likely kill Tray and take her away and would Patrick even care enough to come after her then? Could any of them stand against Weston?

She knew there was nothing in the room to use as a weapon. But she was a weapon, she reminded herself, unfortunately she couldn't turn into it right now. She was stuck in this stupid weak human form. She missed her teeth and claws and...

Claws! She looked at Tray, an idea forming. A crazy idea but it might be the only thing. The men were stuck in human form too, aside from Tray. Brody said he had to get across the road to be able to change so the power of the Stone was limited to a pretty close distance. If she bought herself enough time to cross the street and she came back, she could tear out some throats.

Except they had guns that they had already proven were capable of taking down a werewolf.

No, she couldn't risk them seeing her coming. Her only chance would be taking them by surprise.

She sat on the bed next to Tray and stroked his fur down his back and to his hip. Down his leg to his big back paw. Her finger hit lightly on his claws there and she bit her lip.

Could she?

She pulled his leg up and inspected the claws there. They were long, each one about three inches and sharp as a razor. She looked at his face, still deep in sleep. He hadn't even jerked when she'd touched him. Just to make sure, she bit her lip and poked his healing wound.

Nothing.

"I'm sorry, Tray but since you're not waking up, I have to save us," she whispered. Then she grabbed a towel from the bathroom and wrapped it around the claw to keep it from damaging her hand. She gripped it and stood over him. One hand on his foot to hold it steady and one around the claw, she watched his face for any sign of waking and she yanked with all her might.

The sharp crack of the claw breaking off was accompanied by a jerk and huff from the sleeping werewolf. She didn't move for a second, worried he was about to wake up and attack her for hurting him. He didn't move again and soon was breathing steadily once more.

She unwrapped the towel and nearly giggled with delight. There was one long, sharp, and a little bloody, claw. The next man to walk through that door was getting his throat slit.

Lilly used the claw to slit a strip of towel and wrapped it around the base of the claw so she could have a good grip, then decided to dampen the towel so she could get it even tighter and prevent slipping. When that still felt a little unsure, she cut another strip and wrapped it around her hand with the claw between two fingers. In the end she had a confident weapon and she positioned herself next to the door. No matter who entered, she was going for the throat, and she was not taking chances, she would go for the kill.

She looked over at Tray's still-sleeping body and felt an over-whelming protectiveness. He was hers and they had hurt him.

She didn't have to wait long. She heard a car pull up and the engine shut off then voices as Brody reported what had gone on and that Patrick was on his way.

Lilly stood near the wall beside the door, tensed and ready to strike. She hoped Weston would be the one through the door, if she took out their alpha they were more likely to give up.

She heard footsteps, Simon's door opening, and then the handle of her door turned. Without thought or hesitation she lashed out when the door opened and a shadow appeared there. Blood spurted forward and the man gurgled, eyes wide. He clutched his throat helplessly and fell to his knees. Lilly pushed him forward, then grabbed his feet, turning him so she could shut the door.

She was panting and her heart was going wild. She still gripped the makeshift weapon and looked down at the man she'd killed.

Brody.

"Damn," she whispered. It wasn't the best, but it was one less of them. She managed to drag him between the beds so he wouldn't be visible from the doorway and hoped that the smell of fresh blood and death would help Tray wake up faster. Then she went back to her position by the door.

Fifteen minutes later she heard the other door open and grunts and voices as they apparently carried the injured Simon to the car.

"Go get Brody, what the hell is taking so long?" Weston ordered someone.

Lilly tensed by the door again, lips pressed into a firm line. She knew she had to do more this time, she had to take them all out. The door opened and she lashed out just like last time. It was almost too easy, and the werewolf went down in a spray of blood with a silent scream. She leaped over his body then and ran for the surprised werewolf by Weston's car. She managed to take him out with a quick slash before Weston realized what was happening, but he was on the other side of the car and he had a gun.

"You bitch!" he yelled and started shooting.

Lilly dropped to her knees and scrambled to hide behind the tire. She wouldn't lose now.

"I like your fight, but you're working for the wrong team," Weston said quietly. "I'll make you queen."

"I would never sit beside someone like you, Weston," she snarled.

He was moving, she could hear the crunch of his feet. She moved too, scrambling to the front of the car as he moved to the back. He couldn't get a shot at her with the car in the way, but she couldn't slash at him either. She was going to have to take a leap and hope she could get a better swipe in before he shot to kill.

"I don't want to hurt you, but I will," he warned.

"Which is why you are a crappy alpha," she called back.

The noise should have drawn attention she realized and took a moment to look around, no one was coming to look, no one had when they'd shot Tray either.

"You killed everyone in the motel," she said in realization.

"Humans barely register on my radar, and we didn't need any interference if you made a fuss. Obviously, I wasn't wrong to assume that you were going to cause a little trouble."

"You're a monster," she said, moving to the side of the car as he rounded the back to the other side where his man lay dead.

"Aren't we all?"

"No," she said firmly.

A shot fired and hot pain hit her ankle. He'd shot under the car! She fell back, grabbing the ankle to stop the bleeding. A howl ripped through the air nearby and Weston cursed, jumped in the car with his injured packmate, and drove off.

A black wolf was suddenly standing over her and she lashed out with the claw, scrambling back in fear.

It shifted quickly and she realized it was Patrick.

"Oh thank the goddess," Lilly whispered.

"What happened, where's Tray, are you alright?"

She just pointed to the room where Tray was healing and Brody was dead. "I'm okay," she whispered. "I killed two of Weston's men in there," she shook her head. "He was working with Weston, I'm sorry, I had to."

He gave her a worried look then went into the room. She heard him curse, "Brody you bastard."

When he walked back out his face was twisted in anger. "I should have realized he was compromised," he said with a growl.

Lilly shook her head, a bit frightened by his scowl. "He hid it well, that's not your fault."

"I'm the alpha, everything that happens in this pack is my responsibility. Can you stand?"

She nodded but he helped her anyway. "Thank you," she said and leaned into him as they shuffled along toward the room.

"Of course, Lilly. You're a part of the pack until you tell me you're not, and I take care of my own." He helped her to sit on the bed beside Tray.

She shivered as her adrenaline subsided. She couldn't believe what she had just done. She looked down at the bloody claw still attached to her hand.

"I had to take Tray's claw," she whispered. "It was the only way, Weston has the Stone, I couldn't shift."

"It's okay," Patrick said calmly and squatted in front of her. "Can I look at your ankle?"

She nodded. "At least it's the same one I twisted earlier, so I still have one good ankle to walk on," she said with a hysterical laugh.

"Don't go into shock, we need to get Tray and get out of here. I left my car a few towns over, so we are going to have to take one of the cars in the lot. I don't want to be around when the humans come to investigate this mess."

"Okay," she whispered and looked down at Brody's body. This would be written off as a mass murder, no one would guess that it was a werewolf war.

"Do you know who Weston is?" she asked, meeting Patrick's gaze.

He nodded. "I wasn't sure until I saw him today."

"Why didn't he stay and fight you?"

Patrick took a deep breath. "He is my grandfather."

Lilly's eyes went wide as she tried to piece everything together. "Your grandfather is Gilead! Why didn't you say anything the other night when we were reading the story?"

"I never wanted to use my patronage as a means to hold power, Lilly. Unlike my grandfather, I wasn't raised to rule with force and power, my father rebelled against that and raised me to be a different kind of alpha."

"Is that why he hasn't challenged you directly?"

"I think so. He will though. I stand in his way and if I continue to refuse to join him, he'll come after us to get what he wants. He came through a few years ago and killed an entire clan of Descendants. I told him if I saw him in my territory again I wouldn't hesitate to attack. He sent a group to spy and they almost killed Sorcha, that's when Tray joined my pack."

Lilly nodded at the familiar story.

"So what now?" she asked.

"He has the Stone and he headed back toward Miami. We prepare to defend ourselves and the innocents in our territory. Wait here," he ordered, then left the room. He was back minutes later with a first aid kit. "Found this in the office."

The first aid kit wasn't much, but it was enough to clean and wrap the wound. The bullet had passed through so it would heal fast.

"You're a great alpha," she said when he was done.

He sat back on his heels and looked up at her with a pained smile. "Sometimes I wonder if I'm cut out for all this."

"You remind me of my father. He never left a man behind either. Treated everyone like family and they respected him for it. Weston has nothing to offer werewolves except surface happiness and even if they think that's what they want, he'd never be able to hold a pack together under the conditions he's creating. He's a power-hungry werewolf with a god complex."

Patrick smiled at her and stood up. "Thank you, I needed that pep talk."

Twenty-Five

TRAY WOKE SLOWLY. He was in a car, and he was in his human form. He drew in a cautious breath, not wanting to alert anyone to his state of awareness if he was captured.

The scent of Lilly filled him, and he wanted to leap up and draw her into his arms, but he didn't know they were safe yet. He searched the other scents in the air and when he picked out Patrick's and no other wolf's he opened his eyes.

He was in the back seat of an unfamiliar car, Patrick was driving, and Lilly was in the passenger seat. He smiled and sat up.

"We survived! How the hell did we survive?" His body protested a bit as he moved but he ignored it.

Lilly turned around with a huge smile on her face, "Tray," she said excitedly and crawled between the seats and into his lap.

He held her tight, breathing her in as she trembled against him.

"What's wrong," he said, pulling her head back so he could look into her face. Tears were streaming down her cheeks. "Babe," he whispered.

"I'm so sorry I had to hurt you, I thought you were going to die, and I was going to be Weston's slave and I never would have been able to tell you that I want you and Patrick's pack and all of it. I really do," she hiccupped, and more tears fell.

Tray's heart exploded as her words settled over him. He pulled her face to his and kissed the tears on her cheeks then her lips. He pulled her tight against him and let her tremble as she settled. His gaze met Patrick's in the rearview.

"What happened?" Tray asked.

Patrick just shook his head. "I was too late. She saved you."

Tray stroked her hair and waited for her to be ready to talk. When she told him the whole story he wanted to rage and kill, but it seemed she'd done most of that.

"I am so sorry I hurt you," she whispered.

"You did what you had to do. I would willingly give you anything, you know that." He looked down at his foot. His left big toe was missing the nail, but it would grow back. If his body wasn't so busy trying to heal his other wounds, it probably already would be back. And if it never returned, it was just a memory of what a fierce mate he had and how she'd risked so much to protect them both when he couldn't.

"Weston is still out there with the Stone," Tray said with a heavy sigh.

"He headed east when he took off out of the lot. I'm guessing he went back to Miami," Patrick said. "He thinks he has the upper hand with the Stone, and he wants my pack."

"He thinks he can still win." Tray shook his head in disbelief.

"I'm calling in the pack," Patrick said. "We need to be together on this and root out any of Weston's men he left in the area."

"And make sure no one else fell victim to his promises," Tray pointed out, his thoughts dark as they remembered Brody's treachery.

"He thinks he has an advantage with the Stone, but I think Lilly proved its biggest weakness. Stuck in human form you're no match for a wolf's claws and teeth," Patrick said. "Even the son of Gilead can't survive that."

Tray grunted and rubbed a hand down Lilly's back. "The rumors are true?"

"And he's my grandfather, but my father didn't believe in the way he runs things and neither do I. Werewolves aren't meant to rule the world, we are meant to protect the innocent."

"I only see goodness in you, Patrick. It's why I accepted you as my alpha," Tray said.

Lilly rested against Tray the entire drive back to Miami. If she had the choice, she would never leave his side again. It helped that he didn't seem eager to move away from her either.

When the city was on the horizon, she started to get nervous. The entire pack was going to be meeting them and they would go through the city together, half of them wolf and half human so they were able to deal with whatever they came up against with Weston.

"Don't be nervous," Tray whispered as they pulled off the highway.

"I can't help it. Meeting new wolves has rarely been a pleasant experience for me."

Tray growled.

"Everyone knows about you now, no one will be surprised, and they also know that you are attached to Tray," Patrick said cautiously. "They won't cross him."

She gripped Tray's arm tighter. "Very attached," she agreed.

"Mated," Tray said firmly.

Lilly didn't deny it, but it wasn't really official until the alpha blessed the union and it just didn't feel like the right time. Maybe if they survived the night.

When they stopped just outside the city there were already five cars parked and at least fifteen men standing around.

"Looks like most of them made it already," Patrick said.

Patrick parked and everyone stared as they got out of the car. Lilly held her head high but kept a hand on Tray's arm. There were curious faces and friendly smiles. No one came forward to shake her hand which she appreciated. Patrick greeted each man by name and shook hands thanking them for being here.

Two more cars showed up during that time and added five more wolves to the group.

"This is our newest pack member, Lilly," Patrick said finally and motioned to her.

She cleared her throat and stepped forward slightly. "Hello, I am honored to be welcomed into Patrick's pack."

"Happy to have you!" someone called from the group and the rest agreed heartily.

Tray moved forward and put a possessive hand on her back as the rest of the pack stepped forward to shake her hand and introduce themselves. It was a blur. She'd never remember their names at this point, so she just smiled.

"You lucky bastard," one wolf said as he shook her hand, eyes on Tray. "I guess I'll have to tell Cecilia that her sister is out of luck, you're taken."

"Very," Tray agreed with a growl that made the man laugh.

"Tray is a good man," he said to Lilly. "My name is Robert. I've been in Patrick's pack almost as long as Patrick's been alpha."

"It's nice to meet you, Robert."

Lilly was pleasantly surprised at the lack of interest in her as Patrick quickly settled into giving orders and describing the plan. She felt safe and welcome with these werewolves. It wasn't a trap, it wasn't a cage, it was family, she could feel it.

"Where's Dallas?" she whispered as Patrick talked.

"He's still guarding Brandon at the shop. We'll deal with him after Weston is taken care of."

Lilly nodded, she wasn't sure what she wanted to do with him, but knowing he was in that cage was very satisfying for now.

Half the pack shifted to wolf form and the other half were armed with guns. They would go through the city in teams, and they would take out any werewolf from Weston's pack without mercy. This was war and too much was at stake to give second chances.

"I'm with you two," Robert said cheerfully. "Do you want to wolf, Tray, or want me to?"

"You wolf. Lilly and I will take guns," Tray said.

"Oh I don't want a gun, I don't know the pack well enough to trust myself," she said nervously.

Tray laughed. "Okay, just stay close," he ordered.

That wouldn't be an issue. She gripped the claw in her pocket, she wasn't unarmed. The plan was similar to what they had done before, crisscrossing the city in search of the enemy and working in teams. After an hour they caught scent of vampire and Lilly's instincts rose.

"Doesn't have to mean enemy," Tray reassured her. "But be cautious."

A vampire with a blond mohawk appeared before them. "Why is my city overrun with werewolves?" he demanded.

"Your city?" Tray challenged and beside him, Robert growled.

"My city. I keep the peace here and watch the shore between Atlantis and the humans. Why are the wolves descending?"

"We don't want your city, we are hunting a pack that's come into our territory," Tray explained.

"I thought I smelled something different in the air. My coven won't interfere as long as you are out by tomorrow night."

"We have no desire to stay in vamp territory," Tray assured the vampire.

The vampire nodded and disappeared with a speed that was hard to track. Lilly realized she was gripping Tray's arm tightly and her other hand was wrapped around the claw.

"I don't like bloodsuckers," Lilly whispered. She felt vulnerable in human form.

"They aren't as bad as the Aristotle Society would have had you believe," he said with a shrug. "I've seen werewolves do worse."

"Me too," she agreed with a shiver.

They continued on. When they came to the park where Tray had been attacked last time, they paused and moved forward cautiously. Robert went ahead sniffing and growling. Something was here.

Tray motioned for her to stay back.

She slunk to the shadow of a tree and watched as the men circled the park.

"Don't move, bitch."

The voice sent chills to her soul. The jab of a gun to her side made her stiffen and she didn't dare disobey.

"Weston, don't you know when to give up?" Lilly growled.

"Why would I give up? I found the prize." He stepped back, pulling her with him. "I knew you guys would come back here, all I had to do was wait."

Lilly went along with him, what choice did she have? If she fought him now, he could shoot to kill; her, Tray, and Robert.

Weston dragged her back until they were out of sight, then he changed his grip, grabbing her by the arm and running. She stumbled, her ankle still sore, but he had no mercy and he didn't slow. She fell to her knees once and he merely dragged her a few paces before she managed to get back to her feet.

Tray would know what happened. He'd smell Weston's scent mixed with hers. He'd know that she went along because she didn't have a choice. All she could do was wait for another opportunity to escape and she'd die before she'd let him get her in a car again. She had a lot of hope as long as they were in the city.

A howl ripped through the air as he shoved her toward a car. Tray and Robert were close, she could feel it, but they were being cautious, no one wanted to make a deadly mistake. She expected it but it still twisted her gut. She wanted to see Tray now. Wanted him to dive from a shadow and tear apart this man once and for all.

"Where are you taking me?" she demanded, dragging her feet.

"A little pawn shop I know of. There's some good silver chains I can use to keep you under control better," he laughed. "At least until I can convince my grandson that he's on the wrong side."

She almost grinned and she stopped fighting as he pushed her at the passenger car door. Perfect.

Twenty-Six

WESTON PARKED behind the pawn shop, and she didn't even fight back as he led her inside. She could smell Dallas, but she didn't see him. She could also smell Brandon, but it was different. It was Brandon as a werewolf and that thought tripped her mind for a second.

"You really think some silver chains are going to hold me? I killed three of your men."

"They were unprepared for a woman to fight back. I'm not," he said, jabbing the gun into her side.

"Because you have a gun, that's not really a fair fight," she pointed out, knowing Dallas was inside and close enough to hear. She wanted him to know the full situation.

"I'm alpha. I don't need to fight fair. I need to rule."

"You're an asshole," Lilly said. Out of the corner of her eye she caught movement. She needed to keep him talking, keep him distracted.

"Yeah, you should think about how you talk to your alpha and mate."

"Like I would ever accept you as either."

"Acceptance isn't a requirement," he said darkly.

"See, you're an asshole," she said and pulled at her arm he was holding.

He stopped in the middle of the destroyed store and sneered at her. He pulled her closer to him and she held her breath so she didn't have to take in his hot air. "Call me whatever name you want, darling. You think pissing me off is going to make me get crazy enough to kill you and you won't have to live the life I have planned for you? You're so wrong. My anger will only make your endless life a nightmare for me to enjoy."

She trembled with the desire to lash out with her hands, with the claw she clutched in her pocket but she saw movement and knew Dallas was in position. She had to keep Weston distracted a moment longer. "Your confidence will be your undoing," she said.

He laughed and that's when Dallas jumped, pushing Weston from behind. The gun shot off but missed her and then Tray jumped through the broken doorway catching Weston from the side.

Between the two wolves, Weston was dead in minutes and Lilly was breathing heavy, sitting on the ground watching as the scent of blood filled the air.

Then the howls started. Weston's pack would feel the thread of connection to their alpha cut off and they would scatter. Hopefully they would go back to California and reform with a better alpha. If they chose to stay and fight for revenge, they would die. A werewolf without an alpha wasn't as strong.

Lilly hurried over to Weston's body and found the Stone tucked into a pocket as Tray licked her face with his huge wolf tongue.

"I'm fine," she assured him and pushed his big head away. "But could you go become human again?"

He yipped and rushed out. Dallas sat in front of her, guarding her until Tray rushed back in, naked and human.

"Lilly, I swear I am never letting you out of my sight again," he growled and pulled her into his arms.

"I'm fine. As soon as he told me he was bringing me here, I knew it would be okay. I knew Dallas was here and you'd get to me."

"You are the bravest person I know," he whispered and kissed her sweetly.

Dallas came back in then, human and naked. "We need to let Patrick know what happened," he said and walked over to the destroyed front desk and pulled out a phone.

"Is it over?" she asked, looking up at Tray.

"Just about," he assured her and picked the Stone out of her hand. "This is it?"

She nodded. "The Blood Moonstone. It will allow so much for the pack."

"And us," he said, touching her face softly. "Lilly, I want to take you north."

That shocked the hell out of her. She was expecting him to tell her he wanted to impregnate her right then and there. She pulled back, looking at him with a raised eyebrow. "North?"

"There's something I need to show you."

"Okay," she said, unsure but she had so much trust for him. She was willing to go along with whatever this was.

"Patrick is on the way. Sounds like Weston's pack is mostly running for it," Dallas said, walking back to them and throwing some clothes to Tray.

"What are we going to do about Brandon?" Tray asked, looking at Lilly.

"He's locked up in chains downstairs," Dallas said. "I gave him a frozen steak a couple hours ago."

Lilly shivered at the memories that statement brought up.

"You don't have to stay here. You don't have to do anything," Tray told her.

"I do," she said and stood, looking at the door that led down to that horrible place.

She walked to it, Tray right behind her. He was close enough she could feel the heat coming off his body.

She took a steadying breath then unlocked the locks and walked down. When she saw the small brown wolf curled up on the blankets she'd slept on a million times. She smiled in satisfaction. His body was wrapped in silver chains, and they were already starting to rub through his fur.

"Brandon," she sneered. "How do you like your new life?"

He stood up and growled at her.

"Well, that's not very nice." She walked over to the freezer and pulled out a frozen steak. "How do you like this unsatisfying shit?"

He growled.

She threw the steak into the cage, and he ate it in two quick bites then went back to growling at her.

"If I could leave you here for a hundred years, I would," she whispered. "You don't deserve death, and you don't deserve the honor of being a werewolf." She sighed. "Tray, get me a gun."

The wolf growled fiercely, throwing itself against the cage over and over. It was no use, there was no escape. He knew it and so did she. She wondered if he realized what a mercy this was.

Tray ran upstairs and came back with a gun. He handed it to her. "Silver bullets," he assured her.

"Brandon, for your crimes committed against me and Tray and Dallas, you are sentenced to death. The Aristotle Society dies with you."

He howled as she pointed the gun and fired, four quick shots, then he lay still. His body shifted back to human, and he was just a bleeding skinny man once more. Nothing special, he never was, not really, and now he never would be.

She dropped the gun and stepped back. Tray wrapped his arms around her and held her to his chest, kissing the top of her head. "Are you okay?"

"Take me north," she said quietly. She was ready to move past this part of her life and embrace a future with Tray.

* * *

Tray wanted to whisk her away immediately, but there was a lot to do before they could leave. There was clean up and cover up and a sweep of the city to make sure none of Weston's men remained before they left. Dallas volunteered to stay until sunset to tell the vampires of what had occurred and to let them know that any werewolves that might remain were enemies and Patrick's pack would not hold their deaths against the vampires.

The rest of the pack dispersed before nightfall. Patrick took the Stone. He would head home so he could be with Mary until the baby came. He promised that the stone would be available for anyone else in the pack when they had a pregnant mate due. It would change so much for them all. No more lonely wives giving birth on full moons, no more risky shifting near hospitals to be as close as possible.

It was a gift to the wolves and their mates.

Tray knew everyone expected him to demand the Stone so he could have children with Lilly, but it wasn't the time. He needed her to know him first, and that's why he wanted to take her north. When the time came, if she agreed, he'd ask for the Stone knowing they'd need it for the entire duration of the pregnancy.

They were some of the last to leave the city, Lilly giving Dallas a hug and thanking him profusely for everything.

"Hey, it's what packmates do," he assured her and winked at Tray. "Take care of my brother, he's had a hard life."

"Haven't we all," Lilly said with a laugh.

As they drove north, Tray felt like his life was almost complete. He held Lilly's hand and she drifted to sleep as the sun rose.

Twenty-Seven

LILLY ENJOYED THE ROAD TRIP. She was amazed by everything they saw and enjoyed Tray's company immensely. He wouldn't tell her where they were going, except to say north.

She was curious but she wasn't worried. She trusted him with her life, and any other life they made along the way. Of course he encouraged her to shift and hunt with him often, so she knew he wasn't trying to impregnate her right away no matter how much they made love. She was confused but went along with the journey, he had a plan in his head, but he wasn't sharing it yet.

When they drove into Georgia and she felt a vague remembrance of the area she was both excited and saddened. It wasn't the place she'd known in her youth but there were things, moments frozen in time long enough that she recognized what had once been so familiar.

"I found where your father was buried. I thought perhaps you'd like to visit," Tray explained.

Lilly was too overwhelmed to speak, she just nodded, and he reached across the car, laying a comforting hand on her leg. The connection did help and the knot in her stomach started to ease.

Seeing the world so different hadn't hit her as hard as this foreign feel of a place so familiar.

He pulled into the lot of a cemetery and her heart hurt to realize this wasn't where they had buried her mother. Her father hadn't been laid to rest next to his wife.

It was a beautiful place, she had to admit as they stepped out of the car and she looked around. There was green everywhere, it was well taken care of and lush. Flowers decorated most of the tombstones and there was even a fountain nearby filling the air with the sound of flowing water. Her father would have liked this place and that gave her some comfort.

"Ready?" he asked, holding out his hand for her.

She took it and he led her through the open front gates and along a trail. They passed a few beautiful angel statues and convenient benches. It was a place that welcomed the living, encouraged remembrance, and Lilly thought it was fine, but it couldn't have been what her father wanted.

They'd buried her mother on a hill behind their house, planted a tree and laid a stone to mark the spot. Her father had talked of spending eternity beside the woman he loved, but not until he was sure his daughter didn't need him anymore.

I'll always need you, Daddy, she'd responded every time he talked of such things. It scared her to think of life without him.

She looked up at Tray as they walked and laid her head against his strong shoulder. He wrapped his arm around her and brought her body close to his as they strolled.

Now she couldn't imagine life without Tray. Is this how her mother had felt about her father? Is it why she'd risked so much to become like him? Afraid he would throw her away when she aged and he didn't?

Lilly admitted that the hurt of knowing she hadn't been enough to keep her mother alive was something that ran deep. As much as she loved Tray, and she was realizing it was very much, she couldn't imagine choosing him over a child they might create.

Her father had chosen her, had stayed alive even after she was captured. He had held out hope that she would return, that she would survive.

She had, but he hadn't.

Tray silently led her over a crest and off the trail, up a small hill and to a grave, weathered and a bit dirty.

Tears ran down her face as she knelt and traced the name there. The birth date was fictional to match her father's young face, but the death date made her shudder. He'd lived so long after her capture.

"Did he search for me?" she whispered.

"How could he not have?" Tray whispered back. He touched her shoulders gently. "Lilly there's something else I want you to see."

She looked at him questioningly and he motioned to the headstone beside her father's.

Lilly read the name there twice before she looked up at Tray and back down. "He remarried?"

"A few years before his death actually. No children were born. She was a teacher and when he died, she killed herself."

"She must have truly loved him."

"Life without the one you love is impossible to live," he whispered in her ear and kissed her cheek. "I don't want to experience it without you, Lilly."

Lilly turned in his arms and grabbed his face, staring up into his deep eyes. "I don't want any more days without you, Tray."

"That's how I felt the moment I saw you on Brandon's leash, Lilly." He leaned down and kissed her. "Are you ready to go? We can get a room here in town for the night."

She nodded and he led her back to the car with an arm around her shoulder. She soaked in his body heat, and it warmed her soul. It was comforting to know her father had found some kind of happiness after she was gone. She had wanted that for him.

. . .

A few nights later they stopped in a bustling city, and stood outside a hotel that reached up to the sky.

"I thought maybe we could do something special tonight," he said with a wide grin as he walked her into the lobby. It was so bright and beautiful, all gold and white decorations and it smelled so clean. Honestly a couple of the places they'd stayed the night so far had been barely better than sleeping outside, not that she was going to complain, she didn't have any money to contribute to the journey and she was too embarrassed to ask about his finances.

"This is too much," she whispered as he led her through the lobby to the huge desk where four smiling women stood ready to assist.

"Mr. Jackson, it's so great to see you," a blonde woman with a bright smile and big brown eyes said as they approached.

"We are just heading up to the suite, could you send up some champagne and two steak dinners, rare."

"Right away, sir," she said, and Lilly was pretty sure the woman looked at her with jealousy. Lilly was far too stunned by the entire interaction to react. She just went where Tray guided. When the elevator doors slid shut, she looked up at him and found her voice.

"Jackson? Is that your last name?" She was ashamed to admit she'd never asked, how had she never asked?

"Sometimes it is. I've had to reinvent myself a few times over the years."

"And you're rich," she said carefully.

He laughed and her cheeks burned with embarrassment. "No, I inherited my pack's wealth when the sickness took them all out. I set up funds to make sure that any children of the pack were well cared for and the rest I invested well." He shrugged.

"Does that make you an alpha?"

"It would, if I cared to make a pack I suppose, but I think the time of many alphas is over. The country runs better with Patrick in charge."

"Do you think whoever takes over in the west is going to cause problems?"

"If they do, we are capable of shutting them down. Proven already, so I doubt they'll sneak into Patrick's territory. He comes from a powerful line of werewolves."

Lilly was glad to hear that, she wanted a life of less excitement, at least for a while.

The elevator stopped on the thirtieth floor and Tray led her down a long hallway to a door where he flashed a card over a pad and there was a green light then a click. He pushed the door open and motioned for her to enter.

She was taken aback. It was enormous and open, with wide tall windows taking up two walls. They must be on the corner of the building she realized and hurried to look down, immediately regretted it and scrambled back.

"Afraid of heights?" he asked with a laugh.

"Maybe a little," she agreed. She spun around and took in the rest, a large living room with a huge television and a very comfortable looking brown leather sofa. There was a bear rug on the floor and pictures of various nature scenes hung up all around. The walls were a soft white and gave a feeling of cleanliness that she appreciated. There was a small kitchen area and table big enough for two. Stairs led up to what she assumed was a loft bedroom and from what she could tell, decorated in mostly earth tones.

"How often do you stay here?"

"Not often, mostly just when I'm feeling nostalgic, also I have some business in the city, my investment firm is located here."

"Nostalgic, is that why you brought me here, or is it business?" she asked curiously.

"Both," he said and pulled her to him, capturing her mouth in a deep kiss.

She ran her hands up his arms and shoulders to his hair. Holding him close and pressing her lower body to him as she opened her lips and encouraged him to take the kiss all the way.

A knock on the door broke them apart and she let out a disappointed whine.

"Dinner," he said as explanation and went to open the door.

A young man pushed in a tray that smelled delicious. Her stomach growled and she forgave the interruption.

The boy took the food to the table and laid it out then turned to leave. Tray tipped him and then grabbed her hand and pulled her to the table.

"Food first, then sex," he said with a husky growl to his voice that sent a shiver up her spine.

"I will eat fast," she said with a grin. "So tell me about this place," Lilly pressed as Tray poured her a glass of champagne.

"I grew up north of here. This wasn't a huge city then, but still the biggest around and so I came here as a young man looking for love and fortune."

"Did you find them?"

He frowned. "I thought I had," he said heavily. He looked at her across the table and shook his head. "I didn't know real love until you, Lilly. You are the missing piece of my soul."

"Tray," she whispered and reached across the table to touch his cheek. "You have healed me, I think you know that, but you should also know that I have never felt about anyone the way I feel about you. It must be love because I don't know what else to call it."

"Must be," he said with a wink. "I didn't find real fortune at that time either, but I did okay. Now I'm here with real love and real fortune. So I guess I can finally say I achieved my goal."

"Lucky man."

"Very," he agreed.

After dinner they took the champagne upstairs and Lilly was delighted to see a huge bed. He led her through the bedroom and into a bathroom that made her gasp. A huge tub took up most of the space and she was certain it would fit them both and then some.

"Can we?" she asked with excitement.

"I had hoped you would be into that idea," he said.

She undressed as he filled the tub, adding in some oil that smelled slightly of honey and vanilla. Then he poured them each another glass of champagne and lit some candles before turning off the lights. It was the most romantic thing she'd ever experienced.

She moaned as she slipped into the hot water and laid her head back. "I'm never leaving this tub," she said.

"The water will get cold eventually," he teased as he slipped in across from her.

"Okay, but I'm not getting out before then."

"That's fine with me."

They sipped champagne and Tray washed her back, and her front, paying extra attention to her breasts. By the time he declared her clean she was panting with need and ready to give up on the water even though it was still hot.

"I promise you can have both," he said and turned her to lean over the side of the tub as he came up behind her. He kissed the back of her neck as his hands positioned her hips, spreading her knees apart. His teeth scraped against her sensitive neck skin, and he pressed for entrance.

"Oh fuck, Tray," she groaned, pushing her ass back, begging for him to hurry up.

"Anything for you, love," he said and in one swift push he was buried deep, and water splashed onto the floor.

She almost told him they should get out so they didn't make a mess, but as he started to rock and the water sloshed again, she was lost to the sensations, and she didn't care. His hands gripped her hips, his teeth bit into her shoulder and he took her to the cliff of pleasure and right over before the water was cold.

Then when she was a slippery, satisfied heap, he picked her up, wrapped her in a towel, and carried her to the bed.

"You make me feel like something special," she mumbled as satisfied sleepiness began to take over.

"You *are* something special," he said and pulled a blanket over her and kissed her nose.

She fell asleep to the sounds of him mopping up water in the bathroom and she knew that she loved him more than she had ever thought it was possible to love someone.

Lilly woke the next morning with a burning question triggered by Tray's revelations the night before. She rolled over in bed and found him already awake and staring at her with a grin.

"Do you always wake up this happy?" she asked.

"Seems lately I can't help myself." He kissed her good morning and his hand slipped up her naked body under the sheet.

"What happened to my father's money when he died?"

Tray frowned. "I don't know. If there were no pack survivors to inherit, then it could be sitting in an account still. Alphas usually have a ghost account with most of the assets of the pack held so that there is no reason to change names and inherit as they age out in human years."

"I wonder if I could access it, technically I'm the last of the pack, anything left should be mine."

"True," Tray said carefully.

Lilly could see the wheels of fear turning behind his eyes.

"I would just appreciate having something of my own. I am not looking for a means of escaping you, Tray," she assured him with a smile.

"Good, because I would just chase you down and howl outside your window until you admitted that you do love me and want to warm my bed every night until eternity," he said fiercely.

Lilly giggled and kissed him. "Of course that's what I want."

"Then I'll ask Dallas to look into it, he's good with that sort of thing."

"Thank you."

"Anything for you, love," he assured her and trailed kisses along her face and neck down to her breasts which were already tingling with awareness.

"Sex before breakfast?" she teased.

"Sex, always," he growled, the sound sending shivers of delight through her body.

Any idea about breakfast was out of her mind for the next hour.

The next day they went to a cemetery outside of town and she thought she was finally going to know what this trip north was all about. He held her hand and walked through to a headstone marked *James Steven Bromine*.

"I had a son once," he said quietly. "He didn't know me, didn't know what I was. His mother was pregnant when she left me. I revealed to her what I was. She would only see a monster in me."

"Oh, Tray," she whispered and rubbed his arm soothingly.

"I watched him from afar. Watched him grow, marry, have children, and grandchildren. I watched him die and I knew he had lived a happy life. I knew that I couldn't have given him anything better. His mother was right, I was a monster, and they were better off without me."

"No," Lilly whispered and grabbed his face, pulling him down for a kiss. "You are a wonderful, honorable man, Tray. He would have loved to know you."

He smiled and touched her cheek. "I am a monster, we all are. Humans, vampires, witches, werewolves. We all have something terribly monstrous inside of us that we can let take over. She didn't think I could resist it and for a long time, I would have agreed."

"I don't see anything monstrous in you," she said.

"When I first saw you, I saw a future that I'd given up on. A future that no monster would have a chance at, and I thought if I could have that, it would prove that I wasn't a monster. I know I came on strong, I know that I pressured you to be mine and I would understand if you wanted something else. But I want you to know that there is nothing in the world now or ever that I want more than you, a life with you and hopefully someday, a child with you."

"Oh, Tray," she gasped and pulled him down for a passionate kiss. "I want all of that. I told you I want all of that."

"But that was in the middle of chaos. I needed you at peace telling me the same thing."

"Is that what the road trip was for? You wanted to give me a chance to change my mind?"

"That and I wanted you to know my past. To know why I came on so desperately for you."

Lilly looked at the headstone and traced the name. "James would have been honored with you as a father, Tray. His mother was the only monster." She looked at him and smiled. "Our children will grow up knowing their father is a powerful, wonderful man, and werewolf. You can tell them tales of their lost brother, too."

Tray pulled her into a tight hug, breathing her in and laying a kiss to her neck. "I don't deserve you."

"Yes, you do," she assured him.

Twenty-Eight

TWO MONTHS later they were back with the pack. Patrick was holding his infant son and Mary was happily cooking in the kitchen.

"Was it terribly painful?" Lilly whispered to the woman.

"The birth? I think it's not as bad as the change, or so Patrick keeps telling me when I complain," she said with a laugh. "You should have no problem," she said meaningfully.

Lilly laughed. "Tray and I decided to wait a year, then try." It was still an unknown, both the ability and what it would be born as.

Dallas walked in with a grin on his face. He went to the child first, cooing at it happily, then kissed Mary's cheek and gave Lilly a friendly pat on the shoulder. She wasn't big on affection from the other werewolves still, not to mention Tray growled at anyone who got too close to her.

"I have good news for you," he said brightly.

"About my pack's assets?"

"This is your pack," Patrick mumbled but didn't look at her. It was a discussion they'd had before. She was happy to be a part of

Patrick's pack, but she would always feel a tie to her father's pack, even if she was the last surviving member.

"Looks like he had it all held, tight as shit, too, started under the name Brad Gelsen."

"Hmm, that name does sound familiar. I think I remember him mentioning it."

"It is a ghost account, so it's attached to a number and anyone with that number has full access."

"What's the number?"

Dallas shook his head. "No one knew but him."

"Damn," she hissed.

"All properties were seized by the government when he died, and no one stepped forward to claim them. The bank account though will sit there for eternity until it's claimed, that's the way those things work. So if you can ever figure it out, you'll probably be wealthy."

Lilly sighed, disappointed. "I guess I'll have to get a job."

"Or you just settle into being a housewife," Tray said. "Take care of the kids," he whispered in her ear.

She kissed him, a grin on her face. She could probably be satisfied with that, at least for a while.

"Get a room," Dallas teased, and Mary smacked him with a hand towel playfully.

The phone rang, breaking the moment and Patrick answered it, having no trouble balancing the infant and phone. He was already a great father.

"Katherine, Ian let you up?"

Tray's head perked at the words and Lilly turned to look at Patrick as well.

"I had no way to contact you and tell you, we found the Stone," Patrick told her.

Lilly met Tray's gaze and grinned.

Patrick frowned as he listened on the phone. "No, we haven't been that way in months. Since the monsters attacked."

"Yes, we'll be careful." Patrick hung up the phone.

"What is it?" Tray demanded.

"Katherine said that the Miami vampires are missing, and the Descendants' compound is empty," Patrick explained.

"What the hell?" Tray said.

"She wanted to warn us, and I think she wanted to see if it was us," Patrick said.

"Why would we go after the vampires and the Descendants?" Lilly said with confusion.

"Why would anyone?" Patrick said with a shrug and looked down at his son. "If Weston wasn't dead, I'd blame him. There's no way anyone from the west has come through though, we've been vigilantly watching them. I think we should alert the pack to this development. No harm in being extra careful around here too."

Lilly went to stand with Tray and held his arm, glad she wasn't alone. The pack would come together, and they would stay safe and stand against any enemy.

Tray put a hand on her back, and she felt loved.

"Dinner," Mary proclaimed, and Lilly felt at home.

Epilogue

KATHERINE TURNED to Ian who was scowling. "That sounded like true surprise to me."

"If it wasn't the werewolves, then who the hell was it?" Ian hissed.

They were standing in the middle of the Descendants' compound, and it echoed around them with emptiness.

"And where's the Descendants' Stone?" Katherine met Ian's gaze and they both frowned. Whatever had gone on in the last few months, it was bad, and it was definitely Ian's problem. "I guess we won't be hurrying back to Atlantis like you thought?"

Ian's scowl deepened. "Something has happened to the vampires and the Descendants and you think I'm going to let you gallivant around up here?"

"You saying you can't keep me safe from all the things that go bump in the night, Ian?" she teased.

Ian grabbed her and pulled her tight against him. "You are too important to me to risk, Katherine."

It was a familiar argument, and she knew the best way to stop him from going down that road. She kissed him, slipping her tongue deep into his mouth and slid a hand down to his leather kilt. She knew he was naked beneath it, and she loved that about him.

He didn't want her to be in danger, but he wanted to be away from her even less and that would get him to agree to let her stay above the waterline while he figured things out. She just might have to keep reminding him of it though, which was no trouble at all.

She giggled as he swept her into his arms and walked to a couch, laying her down and stripping his kilt off in a swift motion. She shimmied out of her shorts as quick as she could and welcomed him into her body, between her thighs and the vein in her neck. Spirals of quick hot passion moved through her, and she was arching against him in no time. "Ian, fuck, yes," she gasped as his hips pounded and he threw his head back, his body spasmed in her, meeting her orgasm perfectly.

When he collapsed onto her, she smiled and stroked his back. It was impossible to measure the amount of love she had for this man.

"You'll stay close, and I'll get you a gun," he whispered, then leaned up and looked into her eyes. "You will always be as safe as possible."

"Always," she agreed. "Besides, I promised Felix I would try and bring him some cool things from the modern world, I need time to collect." Felix had become her easy best friend since she'd decided to stay in Atlantis, and the man loved everything she told him about the world above the waterline. She would hate to disappoint him and return empty handed.

But it wasn't a pleasure trip. She looked around the empty room. What had happened here?

"Who's Fray?" she asked, spying some writing on a wall.

"Hm?" Ian asked and followed her pointing finger. "Fray's revenge," he whispered, reading the words scrawled in what looked like blood. "Fray was Sparah's mother. I think they wanted me to find this." Ian hopped off the couch and walked to the wall.

Katherine pulled on her shorts and joined him as they stared at the writing. "What does it mean?"

"It means that we might all be in serious trouble, both on land and in Atlantis."

"Do we need to warn Sparah?"

"Gods I hope it's not too late for all of us," Ian hissed.

Fear trickled through Katherine, and she grabbed onto Ian's arm for comfort. She didn't know what was going on, but she'd never seen Ian so worried.

Please Rate and Review

We hope you enjoyed
Aristotle's Wolves, book two in the Atlantis series, by Courtney
Davis.
If you did, we would ask that you please rate and review this title.
Every review helps our authors.

Rate and Review: Aristotle's Wolves

Meet The Author

Courtney Davis is an author, mother and teacher living in North Idaho. She enjoys sunshine and fresh air, both with a good book in hand. When she isn't enjoying life with her family she devotes herself to the writing dream. She is never short of ideas, only time.

Other Titles from

5 PRINCE PUBLISHING

Visit 5 Prince Publishing
Christmas Cove *Sarah Dressler*
Composing Laney *S.E. Reichert*
Firewall *Jessica Mehring*
Vampires of Atlantis *Courtney Davis*
Liz's Road Trip *Bernadette Marie*
Back to the 80s *S.E. Reichert & Kerrie Flanagan*
Granting Katelyn *S.E. Reichert*
Ghosts of Alda *Russell Archey*
The Serpent and the Firefly *Courtney Davis*
Raising Elle *S.E. Reichert*
Rom Com Movie Club No.3 *Bernadette Marie*
Rom Com Movie Club No.2 *Bernadette Marie*
Rom Com Movie Club No.1 *Bernadette Marie*
A Crossbow Christmas *Ann Swann*
Hot For Teacher *Felicia Carparelli*
The Happily Ever After Bookstore *Bernadette Marie*
Perfect Mrs Claus *Barbara Matteson*
Princess of Prias *Courtney Davis*

Milton Keynes UK
Ingram Content Group UK Ltd.
UKHW010641120124
435917UK00001B/39

9 781631 123498